West & South West England
Edited by Allison Dowse

Disclaimer

Young Writers has maintained every effort
to publish stories that will not cause offence.

Any stories, events or activities relating to individuals
should be read as fictional pieces and not construed
as real-life character portrayal.

First published in Great Britain in 2004 by:
Young Writers
Remus House
Coltsfoot Drive
Peterborough
PE2 9JX
Telephone: 01733 890066
Website: www.youngwriters.co.uk

All Rights Reserved

© Copyright Contributors 2004

SB ISBN 1 84460 622 8

Foreword

Young Writers was established in 1991 and has been passionately devoted to the promotion of reading and writing in children and young adults ever since. The quest continues today. *Young Writers* remains as committed to engendering the fostering of burgeoning poetic and literary talent as ever.

This year, *Young Writers* are happy to present a dynamic and entertaining new selection of the best creative writing from a talented and diverse cross-section of some of the most accomplished primary school writers around. Entrants were presented with three inspirational and challenging themes.

'Mini Sagas' set pupils the challenge of writing a story in 50 words or less. This style of story telling required considerable thought and effort to create a complete story with such a strict word limit.

'A Day In The Life Of . . .' offered pupils the chance to depict twenty-four hours in the lives of literally anyone they could imagine. A hugely imaginative wealth of entries were received encompassing days in the lives of everyone from the top media celebrities to historical figures like Henry VIII or a typical soldier from the First World War.

Finally 'Short Stories' offered the authors free reign with their writing style and subject matter. All themes encouraged the writer to open and explore their minds as they used their imagination to produce the following selection.

All Write! West & South West England is ultimately a collection we feel sure you will love, featuring as it does the work of the best young authors writing today. We hope you enjoy the work included and will continue to return to *All Write! West & South West England* time and time again in the years to come.

Contents

All Saints Marsh Primary School, Newton Abbot
Jamie Clifford (10)	1
Abbie Gibson (9)	2
Alice Hebbes (10)	3
Amber Head (8)	4
Luke Bentley (10)	5
Hanna Millington (10)	6
Colleen Dwyer	7
Stephanie Rowe (9)	8
Kyle Lyon (9)	9
Amie Johnson (8)	10
Lewis Parker (10)	11
Saxon Bignell (10)	12
Andrew Twine (10)	13
Jake Lofthouse (9)	14
Hannah Armstrong (9)	15
Jack Brain (10)	16

Beaudesert Park School, Minchinhampton
Katie Burridge (10)	17
Katherine Dauncey (10)	18
James Baker (10)	19
Laura Bevan (10)	20
Gabriella Ford (10)	21
Lily Haycraft Mee (10)	22
Nicholas Womersley (10)	23
Kate Knowles (10)	24
Julia Young (10)	25
Gabriella Rose (10)	26
Will Purcell (11)	27
Alexandra Wharton (11)	28
Isabel Tanner (11)	29
Olivia Denman (11)	30
Kitty Graham (11)	31
Henry Marshall (11)	32
Alicia Cardale (11)	33
George Hunt (10)	34
Harry Saunders (11)	35

Georgia Hancroft (11)   36
William Birdwood (11)   37

Bickleigh-on-Exe CE Primary School, Tiverton
Saskia Loysen (10)   38
Bryoney Alford (10)   39
Samuel Dallaston (11)   40
Stephanie McKelvey (11)   41
Layla Yeoman (11)   42
Sophie Carew (11)   43
Zoe Elder (11)   44
Rachel Reed (11)   45
Kathryn English (10)   46
Tom Hall (10)   47
Alex Parslow (10)   48
Hannah Webber (11)   49
Naomi Fuller (10)   50
Beatrice Bowles-Bray (10)   51
Alicia Fotheringham (11)   52
Emma Hird (10)   53
Nathan West (11)   54
Fletcher Coney (11)   55

Bishops Lydeard Primary School, Taunton
Charlie Imhof (11)   56
Phillip Berry-Roper (11)   57
James Auton (10)   58
Grace Jacob (11)   59
Hannah Evenden (11)   60
Natasha Coles (11)   61
Neal Gliddon (11)   62
Jasmine Coles (11)   63
Sam Bromage (11)   64
Andrew Flower (11)   65
Elliot Clarke (10)   66
Adam Sanders (11)   67
Kane Clarke (11)   68
Tom Bennett (11)   69
Daniel Tapson (11)   70
Rebecca Beagle (11)   71
Kirsty Edwards (11)   72

Bledington Primary School, Bledington
- Edina Morris (9) — 73
- Eddie Taylor (11) — 74
- Lucy Jennings (10) — 75
- Jodi Tyack (10) — 76
- Bill Pearson (11) — 77
- Logan Bell (10) — 78

Calder House School, Colerne
- Joshua Charlesworth (10) — 79
- Cameron Dempster (10) — 80
- Kit King (10) — 81
- Benedict Skipper (10) — 82
- William Reynolds (10) — 83
- Harry Oliver (10) — 84
- Josh Walford (10) — 85
- Philip Robinson (10) — 86

Compton Dundon CE Primary School, Compton Dundon
- Alexandra Bearman (10) — 87

Ferndale Junior School, Swindon
- Jenna Griffin (9) — 88
- Rebecca Ruddock (9) — 89
- Alexander Sanchez-Garcia (9) — 90
- Abigail Nicholls (9) — 91
- Charlotte Day (9) — 92
- Samantha Telling (8) — 93
- Nathan Fry (8) — 94
- Amie Hester (9) — 95
- Lauren Haynes (9) — 96
- Danyelle Morley (8) — 97
- David Heskett (9) — 98
- Lauren Tyler (8) — 99

Highfield Primary School, Efford
- Jordan Phillips (10) — 100
- Kimberley Robinson (10) — 101
- Natasha Cole (10) — 102
- Tyler Williams (10) — 103

Curtis Munnings (10)	104
Kyla Bunker (10)	105
Alexander Pearce (10)	106

Ladock CE Primary School, Truro
Caitlin Mulroy (10)	107
Rebecca Trethewey & Thai Batchelor (11)	108
Alex Piper (9)	109
Emily Richards (10)	110
Joseph Moore (11)	111
Steven Pinkerton (10)	112
Ben Palmer (10)	113
Michael Shawcross (11)	114

Marldon CE Primary School, Marldon
Hannah Mead (9)	115
Emma Singleton (8)	116
Courtenay Clarke (8)	117
Frankie Dryden (9)	118
Kalam Uddin (8)	119
Bryony Parris (8)	120
Robyn Engstrom (8)	121

Morchard Bishop CE Primary School, Morchard Bishop
Sam Dyne (11)	122
Loren Eginton (11)	123
Emma Sparrow (11)	124
Jessica Kate Powell (11)	125

Newton St Cyres Primary School, Exeter
Alex Porter (9)	126
Megan Kingdom-Davies (10)	127
Lucy Harrison-Prentice (9)	128
Natasha Richards (10)	129
Charley Finch (10)	130
Nathan Jackson (10)	131
Jennie Cocker (9)	132
Edward Leyland-Simpson (9)	133

Pauntley CE Primary School, Newent
    Luke Hodgin (11)   134

St John's CE Primary School, Cheltenham
    Jordan Louise Morrow (8)   135
    Aston Robinson (8)   136
    Francesca Wallbank (8)   137
    Kerry Palmer-Hadfield (8)   138
    Charlotte Morris (8)   139
    Ella Hargreaves (7)   140

St Mewan CP School, St Austell
    Claire Brooks (10)   141
    George Hyde-Linaker   142
    Jack Tucker (10)   143
    Natalie Keveth (10)   144
    Bethany Scoble (10)   145
    Emily Bell (10)   146
    Olivia Grose (9)   147
    Patrick Nichols (10)   148
    Robyn Parkin-Jones (10)   149

Tatworth Primary School, Tatworth
    Jessica Bowditch (10)   150
    Harry Ingrams & Kyran Parsons (10)   151
    George Bragg (10)   152
    Jessika Chloe Woodman (10)   153
    Sofia Harrington (10)   154
    Mark Ricketts (10)   155
    Holly Adeymo (10)   156
    James Orchard (10)   157
    Nathalie L Knight (9)   158

Threemilestone School, Truro
    Ciara Reddington (11)   159
    Bryony Thomas (11)   160
    Naomi Rawlings (11)   161
    Sanjan Duttagupta (11)   162
    Sophie Hay (10)   163
    Olivia Baker (11)   164

Jasmine Rose (10)	165
Danny Martin (10)	166
Wendy Matthews (11)	167
Milly Trevail (11)	168
Chloe Northover (11)	169
Ross Pascoe (11)	170
Carly Maker (10)	171
Katie Bowen (11)	172
Jake Eells (11)	173
Janie Blair (11)	174
Daniel Wiltshire (11)	175

Trannack CP School, Helston
Hannah Finney (11)	176
Lottie Thompson (11)	177
Olivia Tunstall (11)	178
Alice Furness (10)	179
Victoria Martins (10)	180

Uphill Primary School, Uphill
Megan Jones (10)	181
Belinda Hill (10)	182
Charlie Williams (10)	183
Alex Fry (10)	184
Zoe Scott (10)	185
Huw Morgan (10)	186
Lizzie Duran (9)	187
Bonny Owens (10)	188

Widecombe-in-the-Moor Primary School, Newton Abbot
Patrick Cannon (9)	189

The Creative Writing

Mini Saga

My pen was trembling as I wrote. My handwriting turned shaky as the teacher inspected our work. What was she going to say about it?

Suddenly I realised that the teacher had chosen me to read it out. I walked to the stage. A voice in my head said, 'Run!'

Jamie Clifford (10)
All Saints Marsh Primary School, Newton Abbot

In The Distance

In the distance I saw a stripy animal. It seemed to be walking nearer and nearer. I thought I was seeing things but then I saw the stripy thing had gone. Where had it gone?

I turned around to see if it was behind me, but there was nothing there.

Abbie Gibson (9)
All Saints Marsh Primary School, Newton Abbot

What A Nightmare

Suddenly I woke up trembling like a leaf with sweat dripping down my forehead. I turned over to find someone spooky staring at me. I jumped out of bed to switch on the light. I quickly pushed the switch down. It was furry, I saw my cat near my pillow!

Alice Hebbes (10)
All Saints Marsh Primary School, Newton Abbot

The Mystery Bird

It was a sunny day and I was walking up a mountain. I saw a bird with a white cap, sharp beak, sharp claws and a brown body. I looked in my bird book. On page 51, it showed a picture of that bird and at the top it said 'Eagle'.

Amber Head (8)
All Saints Marsh Primary School, Newton Abbot

Dragon

One morning a dragon appeared out of nowhere and decided to go and eat someone. He flew for half an hour but he couldn't find anyone so he ate 7 birds instead, but they didn't taste right. He went back to his house which was a spooky and dark cave.

Luke Bentley (10)
All Saints Marsh Primary School, Newton Abbot

The Weird Ice Cream

I was coming from the beach because it started to thunder. My ice cream started shaking. I thought my ice cream was shaking because the road was very bumpy. Then kaboom! My ice cream exploded. In all the mess, there was a letter, it said, 'Read this, you'll see something . . .'

Hanna Millington (10)
All Saints Marsh Primary School, Newton Abbot

Mini Saga

My hand started shaking as I asked for ice cream. My belly started rumbling. My heart started beating so fast I nearly fainted in front of a crowd. I went home and had a rest. When I went down the stairs, I saw someone staring at me. Who was it?

Colleen Dwyer
All Saints Marsh Primary School, Newton Abbot

Mini Saga

I was on the dirtiest bus ever. I saw a brown bag. I was extremely nosy that time. I took a seat next to the bag. Opened it, in it was a scarf, but wasn't any ordinary scarf. I touched it, it changed colour. Suddenly . . . What on earth had happened?

Stephanie Rowe (9)
All Saints Marsh Primary School, Newton Abbot

Mini Saga

I went to the park and I played in the tree. I saw the ice cream van coming, I climbed off the tree and I went to get an ice cream, I went back up the tree, my ice cream fell off. All I had was a cone. *Disaster!*

Kyle Lyon (9)
All Saints Marsh Primary School, Newton Abbot

The Magic Pen

I went to the charity shop yesterday. I looked around, I saw this beautiful golden pen. It was only 50p so I bought it. I walked home to show my mum and dad. They were shocked because it looked like a magic pen because it was writing by itself!

Amie Johnson (8)
All Saints Marsh Primary School, Newton Abbot

The Mysterious Outline

I was extremely worried. I was dumped on the beach by a van. The moon was full and shining. In the distance I saw an outline of something, it howled. It came towards me, I was about to find out what it was. Was that what they had spoken about?

Lewis Parker (10)
All Saints Marsh Primary School, Newton Abbot

Where's My Mum?

When I woke up I saw something weird. I thought I was dreaming at first, I got worried. It looked evil, so I sprinted down the stairs. Mum wasn't there. The door handle started shaking so I crawled under the table . . . but it was only Mum coming back from shopping.

Saxon Bignell (10)
All Saints Marsh Primary School, Newton Abbot

Mini Saga

The lake appeared out of the morning mist. I saw a bottle drifting into shore. I picked it up. There was the most beautiful ship in the bottle. I sat down under a big oak tree and opened my bag and sketched the misty lake with the sun beaming in.

Andrew Twine (10)
All Saints Marsh Primary School, Newton Abbot

The Roast Dinner

The morning rose, so did my eyes, I got dressed, then the phone rang. 'Who is it?' I yawned down the phone. It was my mate, he wanted to know if I could go over to his house for a roast dinner. I rushed to his house, dinner was ready.

Jake Lofthouse (9)
All Saints Marsh Primary School, Newton Abbot

Stormy Night

One stormy night, it was just before my bedtime when I heard a knock at the old rusty door of my spooky house. I was just about to answer it but then the phone rang! I quickly changed direction, I picked up the phone but nobody answered. Who was it?

Hannah Armstrong (9)
All Saints Marsh Primary School, Newton Abbot

Mini Saga

I was terrified, terrified of dark but suddenly I fell into darkness. It looked like I was in a scary haunted house. I jumped up and opened the door. Suddenly a bony old skeleton jumped out. I woke up shaking like a leaf. It was one of those scary dreams.

Jack Brain (10)
All Saints Marsh Primary School, Newton Abbot

Unfair

A war is no place for children. A battlefield is no place for me and my brother. It's terrible. It's like watching a horrible horror film but it's for real. They killed my brother. He was young. I'll never see my brother again. Why can't this world be fair?

Katie Burridge (10)
Beaudesert Park School, Minchinhampton

That Pesky Cat!

The black cat sat silently staring into the midnight sky watching something with his big yellow eyes. I gazed out of my shining, double-glazed window. The cat suddenly jumped. *Crash, bang, wallop*! 'What was that?' I shouted with terror.

'That darned pesky cat shattering the green house,' Dad replied angrily!

Katherine Dauncey (10)
Beaudesert Park School, Minchinhampton

The Midnight Ring

Ted Cole went clubbing in Swindon. He was 19. At 11.55 he came out very seriously drunk, waiting for a taxi. Out of an alley came some teenagers, with clubs. They battered him to the bone, closing his eyes, he smiled. The clock tower rang. Ted was dead.

James Baker (10)
Beaudesert Park School, Minchinhampton

The Shadow

It clasped its hand round the door, the world went silent. I could see a quivering shadow with long hairs and the tall outline of a muscular body, I screamed. Then a black hairy foot stepped round the door, next to the body. It was the echo-monster!

Laura Bevan (10)
Beaudesert Park School, Minchinhampton

The Tramp

I am a tramp. All I feel is wet, smelly, dirty clothes. Not clothes, rags. I'm enclosed in nothing but cold, dark streets. What can I do? Nothing. I just depend on others to give money to me sitting on the side of the street. My only hope is God.

Gabriella Ford (10)
Beaudesert Park School, Minchinhampton

Stuck

My heart pounded, I fell from the large oak. Rapidly I got up, to start again. Up I went, clasping the next branch. Finally, I reached the peak, grabbed the terrified kitten and swung onto another branch that lurked below my foot. I leapt down to my feet - both safe!

Lily Haycraft Mee (10)
Beaudesert Park School, Minchinhampton

The Return Of The Vampire

The vampire moved like a ghost into the fear of the night. The vampire turned and with his steamy glowing eyes the figure saw him. The figure stared at the vampire, just a little too late! The vampire in the tail coat walked into the night for his next meal.

Nicholas Womersley (10)
Beaudesert Park School, Minchinhampton

The Man

The man. He is here, once more, I know he is after me, I cannot, I will not give in. He is searching the room next door. I cannot move. He is opening the door to where I am. His knife raised, already dripping with blood from another innocent victim.

Kate Knowles (10)
Beaudesert Park School, Minchinhampton

The Baby

I crept to the cot cautiously, was it a monster? I heard a giggle. I looked into the cot, it was a baby.

As the years passed the baby grew into a beautiful bride.

A year later cancer struck. One miserable afternoon, a black figure whisked her into her grave.

Julia Young (10)
Beaudesert Park School, Minchinhampton

My Balloon

We're at the fête, I've just got a balloon. It's a big pink elephant. That's all I want today. I don't want to do anything except play with my balloon. We walk home. Suddenly it slips out of my hands. I watch it drift away, into the big, big, world.

Gabriella Rose (10)
Beaudesert Park School, Minchinhampton

The Day In The Life Of Father Christmas

Bang! Bang! Bang! I woke up startled. The elves had started to make the presents but I did not want to get up. I was very cosy in bed with my night cap on. At that moment Mother Christmas came into the room. She was a small flat-faced women with big eyes.

I got dressed into my bright clothes. I lumbered downstairs looking at my tummy and wondered if I would get down the chimneys that night.

By the end of the day, the sky was ready and the reindeer were attached. A small green elf walked to Rudolph and lit his nose with a blue cigarette lighter. At that we shot into the black sky.

The second house was small, not grand and the chimney was tiny but with no hesitation, I jumped down. It was fine at first until my feet started to get warm. As my feet got hotter, my face started to feel red. I began to scream. The pain was unbearable, I was on fire! I hit the ground and tumbled out onto the carpets, rolled and groaned until the flames went out. I stood up.

I little girl ran into the room shouting, 'Mum, Mum Father Christmas is wearing black this year.'

Before I knew it, I was getting carted off in an ambulance, as I looked out of the window, all I saw was Rudolph's nose still shining brightly.

Will Purcell (11)
Beaudesert Park School, Minchinhampton

A Day In The Life Of A Surfer

As I was surfing into deep water the sun suddenly stopped glinting in a part of the sea, I thought the sun had just gone but I was wrong. I kept feeling vibrations near my foot. I got up on my surfboard and balanced there, but as I did so the surfboard started to wobble even more violently than before.

The seconds passed as hours, but the rocking was slowly dying down. I saw the flick of a tail as it submerged down into the blackness. I felt a wave of relief and struggled back to the beach. When I had only gone a few metres, the great white struck again even more deadly than before. The sound of the cracking board brought me back to Earth. The cold merciless killer engulfed my body and down we fell into the black pit.

As the lifeguard looked out, he saw a creature break someone's board and pull him into the blackness, he summoned the rest of the lifesavers and they jumped into a motorboat and sped off towards the shattered surfboard. There was a trail of blood sinking down, so one of the lifesavers put on a wetsuit and chainmail so he would not get hurt if the great white shark attacked again.

He saw the sinking body below him and there was a lot of blood streaming from his cut-off arm. The shark had disappeared and the lifesaver dragged him up the beach, but he knew it was too late as the damage was too great.

Alexandra Wharton (11)
Beaudesert Park School, Minchinhampton

A Day In The Life Of A Snail

Right then, I'll put my shell on and go for my morning stroll, so I did but halfway round the tree, I began to feel very hungry so I had to crawl very fast which wasn't my best activity.

After that I went looking for my lettuce and lupine or rather the owner's lettuce and lupine. But I don't care if they're hers, I eat them whether she likes it or not! So when I eventually got there, I saw somebody else had been there already. I was thinking, *are there any left for me?* But what I saw wasn't what I wanted to see. Five snails *dead!* It must be slug repellent. I dreaded the thought of it, it kills you almost instantly. Although it's slug repellent, it still works on snails or anything of the slithery kind.

When I got back home, I had to tell the village the bad news and to warn them off because if I didn't there would be more lives wasted and we didn't want that to happen. The thing that really hurt me was when I told them the whole village turned from happiness to sadness, it was no longer the normal snail village, I had known. It turned into a deserted village, there was no more happiness.

So I set off with my gas mask and some water. I was trying to find a new place to eat lettuce and lupine. That night I knew the village trusted me and they were counting on me to find the perfect feeding ground.

Isabel Tanner (11)
Beaudesert Park School, Minchinhampton

A Day And A Life

I woke up and raced to the surface for a good gasp of air. Soon I raced on to find a school. When I found one, I shot off to find my friend and we played games like tag.

'You're it!' squealed my best friend Tornado.
'Hey I wasn't ready!'
'So?'
'It's not fair.'
'Well you should be more aware.'
'OK.'
I chased my friend, she was actually quite fast.
'You're it!' I yelled.
'It's getting boring,' Tornado moaned.
'Fine, let's go,'

We swam along the surface leaping every few minutes and seeing how high we could jump. When we got to our destination we were both exhausted from showing off.

It wasn't fair because Tornado was a year older than me, but she can't jump much higher.

I bet she couldn't jump as high as me when she was my age. Tornado and I really felt like a nice cold oyster since it was a hot day.

With a splash of our tails we swam off. After a supper of oysters we found a sheltered spot to spend the night.

Olivia Denman (11)
Beaudesert Park School, Minchinhampton

A Day In The Life Of A Mosquito

'On three squad - one, two, three, dive!'
    It is a little known fact, that only us female mosquitoes suck blood. We start in groups, then split whilst hunting. 'Split!' I shouted, giving orders. I was leading the squad.
    I flew out to the left and abandoned my group. We were hunting and it was a perfect day! All the beaches were packed with humans, such tasty but dangerous creatures. I know many friends who have been killed by them.
    I whizzed towards a rather obese woman sunbathing on a deckchair.
    What a perfect shot to grab some lunch, I thought to myself.
    I settled on her plump (but juicy) arm ready for some grub!
    'Ouch!' screamed the fat lady. She lashed out with both her chubby hands and swept me off my perch like a leaf swept by the wind.

Tragedy struck, my wings were broken. Everything around me was blurred, wait, there was nothing around me, except yellow. I was recovering my eyesight and I could see I was stuck in a circular box. I was stuck in a bucket. I was stuck in a bucket with a broken wing. Everything began going blurry again, my eyes were closing, until at last I fell asleep.
    I woke up to hear the sound of panting. Then, a huge blob of saliva dropped down onto my back. A huge retriever stared down at me, with one huge gulp, I was dog food!

Kitty Graham (11)
Beaudesert Park School, Minchinhampton

A Day In The Life Of A Soldier In The D-Day Invasion, 6th June 1944, Gold Beach

The chilling breeze swept in amongst the horde of soldiers, inside the cramped and unpleasant environment of the amphibious vehicle. A soft whispering sound could be heard as soldiers thought about the possible tragedies ahead. While the soldiers were wishing each other luck in any possible way, I crept towards my bag at the far end of the vehicle. After two minutes of treading through the endless rows of soldiers, I finally came across my equipment. I looked at my watch. We were due to land in less than four minutes! I rushed as quickly as I possibly could, stumbling over soldiers once again. Once I got to my post, I realised we were now due to land in two minutes. I looked out the side window, HMS Warspite and HMS Ramillies brushed past my window, sending a two foot wave towards us.

The shore was in sight, with the Germans' superior coastal defence cannons swirling round in all directions. Just before I had time to move, two massive shells smashed beside our craft, sending us crashing into the shore. The amphibious vehicle's door opened immediately, thudding onto the sand, sending mini gusts of it flying everywhere.

The soldiers were surprisingly ready, I jumped outside, firing my Lee Enfield rifle. I was relieved to see that none of my platoon was injured yet. They all made it onto the sand, so now was my turn, my moment of glory . . .

Henry Marshall (11)
Beaudesert Park School, Minchinhampton

A Day In The Life Of Father Christmas

Crash! Bang! At last I had arrived at my last house for this year. I climbed down the chimney and into the living room. Everything was bright and cheery, the Christmas tree sparkled, the stockings were hung up by the fireplace and above them there were two mince pies and a little glass of champagne especially for me - yum!

I stumbled onto the flowery sofa to eat my mince pies and drink my champagne. I felt sleepy and I thought I should go but then I decided that I might stay for a little bit longer and look at the cheery room. I started to drift . . . suddenly I felt a tap on my shoulder, there was a lady standing in front of me wearing a flowery frock.

'Would you like a drink and something to eat?' asked the lady.

'Yes please, could I have a piece of fruit and a drink of something?' I said hopefully.

I flung the presents in the stockings, under the tree and left, I staggered wearily outside to see if my reindeer were still on the roof but I found them chomping on some hay in the shed, so I drifted off in the dawn light, back to the North Pole, back home.

Alicia Cardale (11)
Beaudesert Park School, Minchinhampton

A Day In The Life Of A Soldier In D-Day

The noise! It was the beginning of a very long adventure. Was I ever going to rest, perhaps when I'm dead? I was beginning to wonder how all the fathers were feeling? Were they like me, hoping to see their families again?

It was the 6th June - D-Day on HMS Ramillies. I could hardly believe that only two weeks ago, I was sitting in an armchair with young Katie on my lap. Remembering I was in action I carried on with my duties, but the worry wouldn't leave me. Equipped and ready for battle we all looked forward to when this would be over. I glanced down at my watch, it was ten to six and only twenty long miles left to go. Still there was no sight of enemy ships.

Suddenly our ship sounded the alarm, the back of the boat was hit, it must have been a torpedo not a missile because the radar did not show anything. Everyone was shaking. I ran upstairs to the Captain's room but found him on the floor, he was dead. I went to the radio station, the man in charge was also dead, was everyone dead apart from me? Over the noise, a voice, it was coming from down below. I thought I was in luck, a survivor, but no, it was the wireless, the call was 'State your position'. I hadn't been taught but I had a rough idea of how to use it. I called the closest ship HMS Warspite. Our radar was broken so I couldn't tell them where we were . . .

George Hunt (10)
Beaudesert Park School, Minchinhampton

A Day In The Life Of A Tooth Fairy

My job is more difficult than it looks, well actually I don't have a choice of jobs. I am a tooth fairy, I live off teeth, by eating them.

I was on a mission in my new Toothmobile 252, to have a swap of £1 for Jill's tooth. I approached the house where Jill lives and I searched for an entrance, window shut, chimney free. I shot down the chimney with amazing acceleration and put my x-ray goggles on. I peered in Jill's mouth, it was perfect, no fillings, dental floss being used and toothpaste being used night and day. I noticed a problem, she had tucked the sides of the duvet into the bed, I just kept muttering to myself, 'Just do what I did in the practise.'

So I whizzed over to the bed and tiptoed right down the middle, making sure I didn't disturb her. I extracted every last ounce of magic and levitated Jill. Now, as I am the size of a cotton reel, I put out my crane on my Toothmobile 252 and lifted the pillow.

There it was dazzling right before my very own eyes. I reached into the boot and heaved out a massive £1 coin and placed it next to the tooth, I then took the tooth and plonked it in the boot. I put everything back the way it was in Jill's room, including putting Jill back in bed. I went to sleep and then set my Toothmobile on autopilot for Toothfairy HQ.

Harry Saunders (11)
Beaudesert Park School, Minchinhampton

The Day In The Life Of A Horse

Me and my herd were galloping across the grassy mountains of America, I decided to stop and graze on the luscious grass beneath our feet and drink the thirst-quenching water running down the mountainside. We moved on to find a place to rest for the night, until the morning.

We awoke the next day to start our race to get to the mountain peak. After a good gallop the foals and their mothers were getting tired. We stopped for a rest. We paused and as soon as we started to move there was the sound of someone shouting. A heavy hoof was sounding and I started to gallop and the herd followed me, not knowing what was happening. Soon we became aware of what was happening and picked up our pace. We were getting frightened. We galloped across the grassy plains. The young were starting to get exhausted. They were pushing themselves and the stop wasn't very long. What was I going to do? The rest of the herd slowed, I turned. I started to think up a plan. We needed to go faster, I sounded for a race, the herd sped up, the foals went faster so did the older horses. I looked round to find the people on the horses who were trying to catch us were fading in the distance. They were slowing down - they were giving up. Nobody was following us. They had given up. They were gone. Nobody had been taken away. I had saved my herd.

Georgia Hancroft (11)
Beaudesert Park School, Minchinhampton

A Day In The Life Of The Loch Ness Monster

'La ta ta ta,' hummed John the trout to himself as he bumped straight into a green blob. Suddenly the blob whipped round.

'Why hello there, what's a small critter like yourself doing in a place like this?' asked the blob.

'I-I'm J-John and I don't know why I'm h-here,' stuttered John.

'Well I'm the Loch Ness Monster and this is my house,' he said pointing to a vast cave.

'Wow!' replied John. 'What a place.'

The next day John woke up and heard someone calling, 'John, John.' John recognised the voice, he went to the dark exit of the cave. 'John, John.' The voice was getting louder.

'Hello Nemo,' John said back.

The two fish swam into each other.

'Are you friends or what lads?' mumbled the Loch Ness Monster.

'We are best friends,' said John.

'How did you get separated?' asked the Loch Ness Monster.

'This is how it happened,' replied Nemo, 'we were trying to find a restaurant, but we could not agree and I got in a huff and went ahead.'

'Ah,' said the Loch Ness Monster, 'an interesting story.'

'Um, Sir, do you have anywhere to eat?' asked Nemo.

'Oh yes, you must be starving Nemo,' said the Loch Ness Monster, 'come on follow me.'

William Birdwood (11)
Beaudesert Park School, Minchinhampton

A Day In The Life Of A Doctor

I get up at five in the morning, put on my clothes quickly, and go down for breakfast. I put on the coffee machine and try to get the toaster to work. I run upstairs to find that I am wearing odd socks, so I rush to change them. I comb my hair, remembering the coffee. By this time it has overflowed, but I don't have time to clear it up. I eat my toast and sip my coffee, then jump into the car. Just before I set off, I realise that I've left the door open. I lock it and drive to the hospital, only to find a body covered in blood, lying in the road. I leave the car where it is and run towards the body, and shout for help. Two other doctors skid out of the main entrance almost tripping over each other.

'Quick, get him in the emergency department - he's been stabbed seven times!'

Soon the police come, which is lucky because a patient is found to have a gun in his pocket. They sure sorted him out.

At about half-past ten, I arrive home to see the coffee mess. I don't clean it up. I change into my nightie and climb into bed.

Saskia Loysen (10)
Bickleigh-on-Exe CE Primary School, Tiverton

A Day In The Life Of The Queen

I am woken up at 6.30am by the royal butler. My maid comes in and helps me dress, today I shall wear my outing outfit, as I shall be out all day. I shall go out riding with my heir, Charles and my daughter, Anne. At lunch we shall stop in the grounds of Buckingham Palace for a quiet picnic.

Charles shall then go off to his charity workshop, while I will be escorted in an ebony-black Rolls Royce to Exeter, where I shall give a speech on honesty and then I shall knight John Tucker, for risking his own life to save others in a great bakery fire. I shall then have a light supper at the Plaza Hotel and have a good night's sleep before going home to see Anne off to Cardiff.

Bryoney Alford (10)
Bickleigh-on-Exe CE Primary School, Tiverton

A Day In The Life Of A Pair Of Trainers

Today is just a normal day on the shelf. The bad thing is all my friends have gone. I'm all alone. I wish someone would pick me up and take me away. I can't wait to get off this shelf! Wait . . .

Wait. Here comes a boy, he is looking right at me and then he looks away. He is looking back at me! He is walking towards me! He is picking me up! He is trying me on! I'm in luck, he is even taking me to the counter! He is giving the money over! *Sold!* I'm outta here!

I'm in the outside world, it's a big place ad I'm finally being used. Argh! I've just walked right through a puddle and I am now all muddy and wet but I don't mind, *squelch, squelch!*

I'm now sitting on a lovely soft and comfy carpet relaxing. I guess that this is my new home then, it is brilliant and I feel as if I could stay here forever and ever but obviously I will have to go out and explore the world sometime soon.

I am going to be used to play football soon but first I am going for a walk in the woods and I cannot wait!

That tickles! I'm getting brushed down! I guess I am going to be used now because I am being put on and I can't wait to see what adventure I'm going on this time.

I'm now in the woods and my lace has come undone but no one has noticed. I'm gonna fall off soon if no one notices and I don't want that to happen!

Oh great! I am now stuck and am falling into a big blanket of mud. I am going down and down, losing sight of the world and the sunlight is vanishing. It's gone! Help! I am now stuck and no one can help me.

Get me outta here!

Samuel Dallaston (11)
Bickleigh-on-Exe CE Primary School, Tiverton

A Day In The Life Of Whiskey, My Dog

I perk up my ears . . . yes, that is definitely someone thundering down the stairs. I bounce around like a lunatic and then suddenly I am up in the air.

I lick the face of the thing (I believe it's a human, but I'm not sure) and get put down again. I bound off to my bowl and the human (?) puts my favourite breakfast in; chicken and biscuits. I gobble it up in record time and then scratch the big, wooden thing. It opens and I run off; nature calls. Then I race around the garden nine times but before I have the chance to get round the tenth time, an interesting scent tickles my nose. I go off exploring but don't find anything. Perfect, now I've wasted half a day. (I could be digging or killing flowers.)

Ooh, goody I can see a big red thing on wheels, bet you I can beat it to the house.

Oh dear, nature calls again. I trot off after doing my business and go inside. I have a good time killing my bone and playing rounders with my ball. After a short wrestling match with the human (?) I settle down. Wow, I'm tired out. Ah that feels good; getting my tummy scratched is pleasant. Ooh, life sure is good!

Stephanie McKelvey (11)
Bickleigh-on-Exe CE Primary School, Tiverton

A Day In The Life Of A Mermaid

I dive into the sea, the cold, sparkling water exploding all around me, thousands of drops shooting up into the air, then slowly beginning its descent.

My long tail glistens in the sunlight from above the water, as I use it to propel myself down into the depths of the ocean.

I head towards my city, knowing where its calm streets lay on the seabed.

I arrive at my home town swimming towards the shining golden palace, set in pearl, towering above the city.

My father, Balzar, meets me at the door, ushering me inside to the glorious splendour. Colourful banners woven in seaweed, glittering seashell decorations, coral furniture, beautiful mother of pearl chandeliers!

Home sweet home!

Layla Yeoman (11)
Bickleigh-on-Exe CE Primary School, Tiverton

A Day In The Life Of A Foal

A few weeks ago I went to this strange new place without my mummy but now I think it's great here. Everyone is kind and I've got lots of new friends. There's a stallion who lives next to me he's my daddy, my mummy told me all about him. He's just how I imagined him.

After the human children come back from school I get galloped around the field a lot, it's very tiring but extremely good fun.

Every morning, afternoon and evening I am fed one scoop of horse cubes, yummy! I get to walk round the yard and play with my friends. My friends are the mummy cow, the farmyard cat and the pet dog and the only one's who aren't my friends, because I'm scared of them, are the big pigs.

I have to go and be ridden now, sorry bye.

Sophie Carew (11)
Bickleigh-on-Exe CE Primary School, Tiverton

A Day In The Life Of A Kitten Named Tabby

I woke up in a strange but extraordinary place with lots of spiky things. I was looking through cross-hatched metal. I was in a cage and I was desperate to get out and explore the kitty heaven.

Finally someone came and let me out into the garden where I saw a trampoline, swimming pool and a slide, this was truly heaven for me anyway.

I started to stroll forward when I tripped over and banged my head on the hard ground. For a minute I had stars flying round my head, so I bashed my head again and they flew away. I couldn't find what I'd tripped over on until I got up and banged my foot (ouch!). It was a metal tap buried well into the ground. I wondered what it was, it was a sprinkler and I thought it was raining so I ran indoors and Zoe gave me turkey cubes covered in jelly (um!) my favourite!

Zoe Elder (11)
Bickleigh-on-Exe CE Primary School, Tiverton

A Day In The Life Of A Hamster At A Pet Shop

There were twelve pairs of eyes that were hooked to my cage. Suddenly this skin-coloured, poking, fat stick was coming straight at me and prodding me.

Then the shopkeeper took a box from the counter and slowly opened the cage door and grabbed me. I screamed as the shopkeeper dropped me into the blackness. I look up and there were little holes, I tried to get out. I was worried I was a goner!

Rachel Reed (11)
Bickleigh-on-Exe CE Primary School, Tiverton

A Day In The Life Of My Cat Tom

No, no, no! I don't want to wake up now, let me sleep. Oh well now Katie's woken me up I suppose I have to go downstairs and acquire some food. (I can't keep time so I don't know which meal I'm eating).

'Miaow, miaow.' Why won't anyone give me meat? I don't want biscuits, I want *meat!* Ahh at last, yum, mmm - tuna.

'Miaow, thank you.' Oh no, here come the kids. I'd better run before they see me. Bother, I've been spotted *run!* Ow! Why won't that cat flap thing open?

Let go! You know I don't like being picked up. This really has not been my day. We're going to the *vet!*

I'm not scared of travelling really, but if I howl I end up being fussed. You see I have an explanation for everything.

We've arrived. I don't like the vet, his hands are cold and he drones on about things I don't understand, so I scratch him but end up being told off. What's a cat to do?

I'm back home now and settling down but because I missed lunch I'm waiting for the barbecue . . .

Kathryn English (10)
Bickleigh-on-Exe CE Primary School, Tiverton

A Day In The Life Of Frodo Baggins

I'm awoken from my broken slumber (I haven't been sleeping well recently, drawn to the power of the ring) by my closest friend Samwise Gamgee. I stretch wearily, it's barely light but still we must continue on our quest. I stand and check, then re-check that we have packed all our belongings, then we set off.

For lunch, our guide Gollum found a freshwater stream and we ate the elven bread from Rivendell.

After lunch, it got dark within an hour or two, so we were forced to find shelter. Sam pointed out a fallen tree, this is where we would spend the night. We haven't travelled very far today, hopefully we will make more progress tomorrow.

Tom Hall (10)
Bickleigh-on-Exe CE Primary School, Tiverton

A Day In The Life Of General Gordon

I woke up to the sound of gunfire and it was close. I leapt out of bed and punched open the shutters.

The Arabs were here in Khartoum! The British were plainly getting thrashed, the Arabs never seemed to stop coming.

Over the Nile into the British and into Khartoum. All of a sudden my heart was racing. What should I do? What could I do? Then I realised I would have to fight to the death but at least only a hero would do that. I was a hero.

Alex Parslow (10)
Bickleigh-on-Exe CE Primary School, Tiverton

A Day In The Life Of A Cat Called Bootze

Ah morning already. Right time for breakfast. Raw rabbit, minced mouse or beheaded bird? I think I'll go for minced mouse, better get there quick, before Tom, my brother, eats them all. Damn, all I can find are bones and tails. That means I'll have to go with raw rabbit. Better get there before Midnight has one or else they will not come out till they know it's safe, that's normally two hours. Damn, not again! There's a dead rabbit in the middle of the field. Okay beheaded bird, the last thing.

I see a bird, it's a blue tit, the fast bird, well to me it is. Crouch position and leap. 'Argh! Help! Help I'm stuck! Help me!'

Ten minutes later. 'Hey look, a man in a hat, why is he wearing a hat? I'm not going to jump or land on his head, or am I?

Finally I'm out of that tree, I wonder what the time is? 4.30pm - oh well I'd better have a kip to get rid of the shock. I bet Hannah will wake me and give me some cat food tonight.

Hannah Webber (11)
Bickleigh-on-Exe CE Primary School, Tiverton

A Day In The Life Of My Deaf Cat Bonnie

Argh! What's that? Oh it's my tail dangling in the slimy, green, wet pit (the pond). Look over there, some fresh food, crunchy munchies and goopy meat, my favourite. Next comes the most *important* part of the day, washing.

After washing comes sleep. I always get surprised and woken up, but not this time, I'm going to wake up when I want and if they even try to surprise me. I'll be ready.

Argh! What is that? Oh it's a person. I never saw them come in or heard them, well I never hear anything for that matter.

Look over there, a nice, warm, *dry* lap, perhaps I could sneak onto it. Hey, why won't you let me on? Okay, I dribble and maybe I'm a little wet but only my tail. My legs and everywhere else are dripping from the rain but that's no reason to reject me. Oh good, you're getting me more food, I'll eat it, then go to sleep.

Naomi Fuller (10)
Bickleigh-on-Exe CE Primary School, Tiverton

A Day In The Life Of A Sock Named Bob

It's the morning! And oh that runaway grasshopper is in good voice. Seconds later . . . stampede! The human beans must be up and about. I am roughly and reluctantly dragged from the line and unmercifully shoved on a mouldy foot. Obviously the word *bath* has *no* meaning here! Oh the shame!

As the day goes on (after being strangulated by those lace-up shoes and covered in multiplying body odour) the smell and wetness results in nausea. The life of a sock is hard.

In the car home . . .

I am being peeled off from a pair of slimy and now quite repulsive 14-year-old's feet! The heads of the giant beans turn in disgust. Well I hardly think it's *my* fault. But unfortunately, the sock is always blamed. And as the car reaches the drive-in; the heavy hand of blame lingered over the dreaded washing mathingy.

Beatrice Bowles-Bray (10)
Bickleigh-on-Exe CE Primary School, Tiverton

A Day In The Life Of A Puppy

Mum, Mum, where are you? Why did they take me away? Mummy why was I shoved into a dark box?

I feel quite ill now being jiggled about. *Creak!* Aarrgghh! Oh my eyes, oh the light. I creep out, scared right to the tip of my tail . . .

Plop! What's that thing swimming in water? Where's its paws? How can it breathe under there? Where's the bone for it to eat?

'Miaow!'

Aaggghh! What's that black thing? Why is it staring at me with those gigantic emerald eyes? Why is it sniffing me with its overlarge nose? Why are its ears twitching eagerly? Why is its tail swinging about in that odd manner? Oh look at its teeth, they're razor-sharp.

'Squeak!' What's that thing that girl's bringing in? It's too big to be a hamster yet its ears are too small to be a rabbit's.

Oh what's going on? Where are my brothers and sisters and where's my mum? I miss her a lot, but maybe this is just a temporary home. Oh but I do like this girl, my fur feels really smooth now. Temporary or not temporary, maybe I'll be able to love these people almost as much as my mother.

Alicia Fotheringham (11)
Bickleigh-on-Exe CE Primary School, Tiverton

A Day In The Life Of A Kitten

At 6.30am I am woken by the baby tugging at my tail. Then I'm given my breakfast, water and a tin. Water! Who do they think I am? A bucket? I like milk. I guess I'll have to try next door, they always have *fresh* fish, not boring old tins.

Now I've finished breakfast, it's the most important part of the day - washing time. I love the feel of my fur going along my tongue.

Now comes tea but where have my humans gone? Here they are but what's this furry cage for? I'll go and investigate . . . No, I don't want to go in the car! Help! Miaow! Not the vets . . .

Well, this place looks familiar but it's not the vets, hey hang on - what are all these cages for?

Don't put me in one and where are you going? Don't leave me here!

Hey what's this? It looks comfy, maybe I won't mind it here.

Emma Hird (10)
Bickleigh-on-Exe CE Primary School, Tiverton

A Day In The Life Of A Buddhist Monk

I awoke to the sound of a cockerel at 4.45am, so I put on my flowing, cotton, saffron-coloured robe and sash and made my way to the temple.

As I arrived, picked up my alms (offering) bowl, walked into the village to collect the donations from the villagers. Today I received two joss sticks, one bowl of rice and a small candle.

When I arrived back at the temple, I took off my sandals, said a prayer and sat down for breakfast at 7am. For breakfast I had a bowl of thin, weak porridge, and two papayas, not a lot I know, but I am still thankful.

After breakfast I said a prayer of thanks then proceeded to the classroom for the first lesson of the day: the ancient language of Buddha: pali. We learn this so that we can read and study the sacred scriptures.

At 11am, we moved to the dining hall for the second and last meal of the day. For lunch, we had fish curry, steamed rice and string beans. We then said another prayer of thanks and moved back to the classroom and learned the theory of Buddhism. By this time it was 8pm, so I said a quick prayer and fell asleep.

Nathan West (11)
Bickleigh-on-Exe CE Primary School, Tiverton

A Negotiation And Retrieval Officer

A definite proof of life was received at 21.00 on 5th May in an isolated Polish village. My people then proceeded to the northern mountain regions. It is there that I will retrieve my cargo and complete my mission.

There are a positive 35 men around a shack in the centre of a clearing. Presumably inside the shack lies the cargo (victim of kidnap). 35 is a large number for 5 men to handle. I fear we may have to be loud. There is one man coming for member 1. The man's down. Member 1 moves for the shack. *Bang!* 5 men down. 31 rifles are being loaded. Member 4 fires a heat-seeker rocket at the mass of men. I move into the shack. I see my cargo waiting. I hear member 5 roar up in a 4x4 with member 4 in the back firing his AK47 at the approaching soldiers. We move out. We have lost a close friend and saved an innocent man.

I'll never think the same way again.

Fletcher Coney (11)
Bickleigh-on-Exe CE Primary School, Tiverton

A Day In The Life Of A Vampire

I woke up in the morning from the dark shadow covering the bed in a sudden jolt. I then stepped over to the hole in the wall, then I looked out. It was the usual. You might refer 'morning' to midnight, of which I make good time. I shut my eyes, then my white skin was covered in the usual black cloak, shirt and robes. I sprouted my fangs . . . time for the normal breakfast-blood.

    I turned the old-fashioned phone on, next to my bed. 'Open the roof up!' I called the second my slave picked up the other side in a yawn. The bricks in the castle roof cracked, then a smooth hole in the roof opened. My heart wasn't beating . . . I was nearly out of blood . . . I must get a move on, fast. I spun around fast, as a throttling web of blackness covered my skin, and turned me into a ragged black cloak, or better known as bat form. I looked in the smashed mirror in the corner of the room, to see what I looked like . . . I looked . . . well . . . weird! I couldn't see myself. The feet, tucked under the cloak, stood on the ground, then, with a brutal kick, I shot up through the roof faster than a bullet from a gun. I hovered closely above the city buildings, at which I flew through a hole in the side of a wooden house . . .

Charlie Imhof (11)
Bishops Lydeard Primary School, Taunton

The Tournament

I must get the arrow in the middle of the red or I am out and I can say goodbye to my head. Everyone was cheering. I loaded, I pulled back the bowstring, I took my aim and released, *zip*, I hit, Whoops that's the sheriff's huge backside!

Phillip Berry-Roper (11)
Bishops Lydeard Primary School, Taunton

The Chase

Its snapping jaws were chasing me! My heart was thumping. I turned my head, it was closer. Now I could just make out its shining claws. It had caught me but I jumped, grabbed a branch and pulled myself up into the tree. This weird creature ran. I'd made it.

James Auton (10)
Bishops Lydeard Primary School, Taunton

A Day In The Life Of A Monkey

I woke up one morning, I wasn't in my bed, I was in the jungle, hanging by my tail. 'Tail! I don't have a tail - I'm a monkey, but, but how?'

I went over to another monkey and tapped it on the arm, it was my brother, he screamed (like a girl).

'You're a monkey too,' I said.

'Don't be stupid!' he said.

I went to explore, it was all still, then the birds suddenly scattered at the sound of a gunshot.

My brother came swinging through the trees calling for me, we went swinging through the trees, till he hit a tree and fell, I had to slap him to get him up.

We slept there that night and when I woke up I was normal.

Phew! Was it a dream?

Grace Jacob (11)
Bishops Lydeard Primary School, Taunton

A Day In The Life Of ET

Flashing lights all around me, the ship is blowing up. My parents will die, we've got to get off! *Jump!*

We are safe, my parents aren't hurt, but they must leave me, men are coming . . . *humans!* They have long pointy things with triggers on them. I think it's their kind of weapon, oh well, I have weapons too. Plasma guns to the rescue! I manage to get away but I drop my guns. I find a shelter from the cold of night. There are lights on inside and weird sounds that make me want to dance, I've never heard this before.

Someone is coming out, it's a human, ugly beasts if you ask me. My parents always said they are pests, full of disease and germs.

I need to get away, I heed to find some things to build a ship and find my parents, but the good thing is I've built a ship out of a thing that blows air. The side of it says, 'hairdryer' and it has loads of parts of metal. I hope it'll reach Jupiter!

I can hear somebody calling my name, it's Mum and Dad, we can go home. *Yes!* I'm chasing my name, I'm getting closer. My parents! I thought I'd never find them. 'C'mon Mum, c'mon Dad, we're going home.' We take off home and make it! *ET go home!*

Hannah Evenden (11)
Bishops Lydeard Primary School, Taunton

Puppy Love

I woke up one morning and found a puppy barking at me madly. I screamed as I wasn't expecting it and then the puppy hid behind the bed. I crept up to the puppy and looked at it. I picked up the puppy from the floor. Could I keep her?

Natasha Coles (11)
Bishops Lydeard Primary School, Taunton

A Day In The Life Of Shrek

I woke up, went to the toilet and then Donkey came along and said, 'Wazon Shrek?'

'Just going to the bathroom, Donkey,' I replied.

So then I went to the toilet and then went to the muddy green sick bath.

'We're on in five,' the director said.

Five minutes passed and we were filming Shrek 2, the funniest, weirdest film ever. After that I got really tired walking in the woods with that cast and that unstoppable donkey. Then me and donkey turned beautiful. I turned into a man and Donkey turned into a stallion!

I went back to bed and there was a wolf sleeping with his white nightgown with red flowers so I got into position and shouted, *'Get up you lazy wolf!'*

So he legged it as far as he could go. By this time I was annoyed, very annoyed. I went to the dining table, picked some earwax, put it in a pot for a candle and then ate somebody's eyeballs and their organs.

Neal Gliddon (11)
Bishops Lydeard Primary School, Taunton

A Day In The Life Of My Dog!

I woke up with 'Misery Boots Kira' and 'Going On Coco'. When my owner didn't come down, we started howling until finally someone came down. They opened the door and before long I was rushing through trying to get in the living room, then I turned to find my owner flat on his face, ha, ha.

The door was still open so I hurried to the kitchen, stamping on his head, but I rushed to lie down and pretend to be asleep.

He came in shouting at me, but I gave him my sweet look, but he put me outside all alone.

I barked and barked and barked and sat down, tongue out, ears down and paws on the door. I must have looked so stupid that when he came to let me in he laughed at me. I was so embarrassed and even Kira and Coco barked in laughter. 'Oh very funny, Warthogs.' That stopped them laughing and then 'Misery Boots' put her huge butt in my face, how gross. Then Coco went on and on and knew I wasn't listening and blew off in my face. All along I was wondering what the smell was. 'Golly Ganges, that smells,' I said, trying to hold my breath.

I went onto my bed and then my friend Jaz came out for her breakfast and gave me a huge cuddle.

Then all the day I slept and snored and had breakfast and snored again.

Jasmine Coles (11)
Bishops Lydeard Primary School, Taunton

The Yeti

I fell down and landed sitting 5 ledges below. Typical. I was climbing Mount Freezer, but I wasn't being very successful. I pulled myself out of the snow and saw a yeti! It ran at me, jumped and flew off the mountain. The yeti was dead. They are extinct now.

Sam Bromage (11)
Bishops Lydeard Primary School, Taunton

The Short Battle Of Hastings

We were on the hill, our feet were painful from marching. Then we heard shouting, suddenly we heard men charging towards us. The Normans lost and ran away. The crowds fired down on top of us and we heard a yelling sound and saw that our king was lying dead.

Andrew Flower (11)
Bishops Lydeard Primary School, Taunton

A Day In The Life Of The D-Day Landings

In the boats we come closer to the Normandy beaches and the fight, bombs are pelting the water, soaking us. We're all ready to fight. With my M1 garand in hand, Nazis will face the fury of the British.

'10 seconds,' yells out the captain. Seconds later, the boat hits something hard, we all jolt forward, water starts pouring in, the front of the boat goes down, the battle has begun. We rush out wading through the remaining water, the bunkers are high, well defended and armed, but we try our best.

Me and a squad of 20 others move into a German trench, led by the captain, we fight well. My best friend, John is with me, he's been shot but I will not let go of him. In the end I let him because I know the Nazis are coming.

Out of the trench and onto the beach we go, firing like mad, my brother, Miles and I, have been assigned to find a way into the bunkers.

We are in, the Nazis are dead, we have cleared the suckers, but it is a time of great sadness for the hundreds and thousands of men who've died. My hands are covered in blood and will never be clean.

Elliot Clarke (10)
Bishops Lydeard Primary School, Taunton

A Day In The Life Of A Yeti

I woke up and walked out of my ice cavern. My stomach rumbled and I went searching for food. I strutted round the giant mountain, my huge feet stomping on the ground. *'Ouch!'* I stood on something. I lifted my hairy foot and under it was a tiny metal clip. I bent down and yanked it. As I pulled it out, loads of rope came with it and, on the end of the rope, were two small, shivering men. I chucked one man in the air and tried to catch him in my wide mouth, but I missed him. The man hit my chest, bounced off and fell down the steep mountain. I was never good at that anyway. I saw the other person sprinting away. 'How dare you?' I shouted, beating my chest!

I snapped an icicle off a rock and started to chase him, smacking the icicle on the ground, but missing the little man. Suddenly he turned into a cave. It was a yeti's cave but I still smacked around with the icicle. All the furniture got destroyed.

Just then I heard something, *squish!* It was the man. I picked him up and chucked him in my mouth, but found out the cave I had destroyed was my cave. 'At least I got the man,' I said to myself.

I went out onto the mountain to find another cave when I did a huge burp. Suddenly a snow avalanche came down and I got crushed!

Adam Sanders (11)
Bishops Lydeard Primary School, Taunton

A Day In The Life Of A Blackbird

I suddenly woke at the break of dawn. I stretched my wings as wide as I could and fell back onto my twigged bed, and I saw my friends fly by my treetop. They were playing a game. I thought I would join in with them. They were playing a game where I had to catch them. But I got tired of that game after a while because we play that game every day. I was tired of flying and racing about. So I perched quietly on top of a high fence minding my own business. Then suddenly a dark ginger cat pounced up at me and nearly grabbed me in his chops. I quickly glided on top of a house roof. The dark ginger cat was staring at me licking his chops.

He suddenly knocked at a long and thick pipe. He slowly pushed his paw onto the pipe, he stepped backwards and pounced forward onto the pipe. My left wing didn't feel fit enough. It was aching like mad. I couldn't fly.

I ran off the top of the roof trying to fly but instead I fell. I was just about to land in the cat's mouth. But just before, my friends pushed me out of the way and held onto my right wing and safely took me back home. And that's my typical bird life.

Kane Clarke (11)
Bishops Lydeard Primary School, Taunton

A Day In The Life Of Frank Lampard

I woke up really early in the morning. We were going to play a match that was so important. If we won, we would win the Premiership. I had just remembered I was going to be captain of the team. I was running a bit late so I jumped out of my bed and hopped into the shower. I always looked smart before every game and definitely the most important ones like this one. I had breakfast. I think being the captain, I am the best player.

It was nine o'clock. It was just about time to meet at the training ground. I said bye to my girlfriend and my dog, Tom.

I was the first one there, waiting until my buddy came, called Damien Duff. I was getting so excited. We finally got there at Old Trafford, it made me feel sick, looking at the stadium.

We had a team talk and then I led the team out onto the pitch. I was pretty confident. In the background you could hear the crowd roaring and screaming. I was leading my team to victory!

Tom Bennett (11)
Bishops Lydeard Primary School, Taunton

A Day In The Life Of A Buzzard

I woke up at daybreak and reluctantly flew out of my cave to hunt. I flew round in circles getting steadily dizzier and dizzier. I saw a speck of brown below and I dived. I hit something hard.

'Ow!' said a voice. 'What are you doing?'

'Pegasus?' I said weakly.

'What?' he said.

'It's your friend, Speeder, come back to my cave and we'll have some cocoa.'

Pegasus thought for a while then he said, 'Okay.' So off we flew talking in Buzzatongue rapidly.

'Why haven't I seen you for ages?' I asked.

'Oh,' he said, 'I've been transferred to another branch.'

I snorted, his sense of humour hadn't changed.

When we got back to my house - a cave in a hill, I lit the fire and made some cocoa.

'Do you want to hear a story?' he asked.

'Yeah,' I said.

'Good, now listen. I was flying at thirty miles an hour when a bird hit me, I heard nothing, I was asleep!'

Daniel Tapson (11)
Bishops Lydeard Primary School, Taunton

A Day In The Life Of A Child In The Blitz

'Goodnight Mum,' I called over the banister.

'Goodnight Sarah,' my mother walked up the stairs towards me, 'get into bed now, see you in the morning.'

I lay in my bed, underneath the slippery eiderdown and scratchy blankets, hugging my knees. It was winter and freezing cold too. I slowly drifted off to sleep . . .

Suddenly a loud siren woke me. I tried to go back to sleep, but it did not go away. Wait a minute, I knew that sound, it was the sound of an air raid siren . . .

Quickly I grabbed my dressing gown, my boots and my puppy and ran for the shelter at the bottom of the garden. I was the first one there, I opened the door and stepped inside.

I lit the lantern and sat down on my stool to wait for the others. While I waited, I thought about tomorrow, *eeuugghh* . . . even the thought of being taken to Wales to live with a family I didn't know sent a shiver down my spine.

'*Argh!*' my big sister Anna's shrill scream put a stop to my thoughts . . .

'Anna! Anna, what's happened? What's the matter?' I yelled as I scrambled out of the shelter.

'I . . . I sa- . . . I . . .' she couldn't speak.

'Have you seen some bombs?' I was frightened now.

'No. I . . . I thou- . . . I thought . . . I thou- . . . I thought I saw a spider!'

'Whatever is happening?' Mother was here now.

'Nothing Mother,' I sighed as I settled down with Barney (my puppy), it was going to be a long night.

Rebecca Beagle (11)
Bishops Lydeard Primary School, Taunton

A Day In The Life Of My Dog Briony

I woke up this morning and got up, my eyes still shut. *Thwack!* I fell off the edge of the bed. I picked myself up and looked around. Master was still sprawled out on the bed. Sigh, I had best wake him up, it was time for my walk. I didn't have to. He stood up and went to the bathroom. I don't know why humans go to the toilet in the water bowl. I bounded down the stairs only to be greeted by a squirming puppy. Then I realised it was microchip day. Master wandered downstairs and let us out. He picked up Bob and opened the gate. I rushed out and ran straight into a tree!

We arrived but I was told to stay in the car. I waited and a little while later came a yelp. Yes, he was officially named. He would come back and go, 'Welcome to AOL.' And when his bladder's full, 'You have e-mail,' when he goes to the toilet, 'Printing started'. Yep all this just cos he's got a computer chip in him.

I stuck my head out of the window. We were on our way back from the vets and Bob was asleep in the footwell. I wonder why they have catseyes? Why not dogs' or rabbits' eyes? Hmmm, something to ask the cat next door.

We arrived home and I settled down for a good long sleep. I dreamt of chasing Felix, pinning him against the wall and asking him if *his* eyes are in the road.

Kirsty Edwards (11)
Bishops Lydeard Primary School, Taunton

My Birthday

I was going to the swimming pool. We were squashed in the back of the car with all of us. Five minutes later everyone appeared we were all sent to the changing rooms to get dressed. We jumped in and started playing with the floats. Trouble. Finally it stopped.

Edina Morris (9)
Bledington Primary School, Bledington

Bees

Running, one way only. Where to go? Nowhere! Swarm, yes everywhere, what could I think of? Nothing. What to do? Just run. What I did, never mind, 5,000 bees I think, left, right and behind, yes not ahead, I don't deserve this - zzzzz! Light and then blackness.

Eddie Taylor (11)
Bledington Primary School, Bledington

Wake Up!

I was asleep in my warm, cosy bed. Suddenly I was on cloud nine! I was in a short, sparkly dress and groovy shoes. I was on a stage singing. My heart was thumping.
　'Wake up Lucy!'
　It was all a dream.

Lucy Jennings (10)
Bledington Primary School, Bledington

Breaststroke In The Air

I couldn't believe I was flying. I was doing breaststroke in the air. Maybe high, maybe low, nobody could see me. I could whizz off or slow down, it didn't matter. I could see them but they couldn't see me. Wonderful. I awoke, I thought it was all so true!

Jodi Tyack (10)
Bledington Primary School, Bledington

The Roller Coaster

Jolt! We're off, up, up, up, up and . . . argh! Down as fast as lighting. Round and round and then whoosh as your stomach turns upside down. Round, up, down, side to side, back and forth then sick out of mouth and *scream, scream, scream!* Stop at last.

Bill Pearson (11)
Bledington Primary School, Bledington

Trick House

I walked into the room and fell down the black hole. I landed on my back in a dark, dusky room, filled with dust. I fell back into an armchair, I was all alone. My throat dried, I felt for a glass of water, it was put into my hand . . .

Logan Bell (10)
Bledington Primary School, Bledington

A Day In The Life Of A Cowman

The cowman gets up a six in the morning to milk his cows. First he gets the cows into the yard and walks them in one at a time to the milking parlour. They each stand in a metal stall and eat cow pellets whilst the cowman puts a special quadruple machine on their udders which squeezes and sucks at the same time.

Beside the cows is a tank which shows the cowman how much mike each cow has produced. When the cow has finished the quadruple machine drops off. The cow walks out of the stall, through the parlour and into the yard.

The milk from the tank gets pumped into a bigger tank. Once the cowman has stopped milking, he cleans the parlour and the pipes which take the milk to the tank. There is a big slurry pump which pumps water through the parlour and takes the dirty water away.

The cowman takes the cows into the field. At nine at night a milk tanker will come and pump the milk out of the tank and take it to a milk factory.

Joshua Charlesworth (10)
Calder House School, Colerne

At Day In The Life Of A Boy At Calder House School

On July 5th, Philip Robinson and some other Year 5 pupils went to Montacute House. First he ran up and down the long drive. Then he went into the garden. It was beautiful with lots of flowers and mown grass.

After that he went to the kitchen where they were told what happened in Tudor times. Girls had to get water from the lake for cooking and the boys had to turn the spit. It takes a long time, twelve hours, to roast a pig.

He then went into a magnificent bedroom. There was a four-poster bed all carved with flowers and animals. Next he went to the sitting room. It had lovely carved animals all round the sides. The dog and the deer were amazing but they had never seen an elephant before, so when they tried to make one it came out all wrong. It looked a bit like a pig with a dog's hind legs. Then the children went into the Great Hall. It had a 3D picture carved in the wall, It looked like a lady was hitting a man but that was unusual because in Tudor times a woman would not hit a man.

The last place Philip visited was the Long Gallery. It was very long, about 52 metres. They used to play games in the gallery when it was bad weather.

After that Philip went to see a portrait of Queen Elizabeth I and he made a miniature of the painting. Then it was time for a picnic and then they went back to school.

Cameron Dempster (10)
Calder House School, Colerne

A Day In The Life Of A Tudor Boy

Kit woke up at nine o'clock in his four-poster bed. It was still and not a sound could be heard, so he pulled back the heavy curtains. The sunshine washed over his face and woke him properly. Then he went to change and dress.

Kit was going down the stone spiral staircase when he met his good friend, Felix, running up. Felix was a servant at Montacute House.

'Your father has arrived and is planning a party tonight!'

'Am I included?' asked Kit.

'Yes, you are going to dine with Sir James at the feast.' Sir James was Kit's uncle and he did not like him. 'Also, you are going to sleep in the barn tonight, there are so many guests!' said Felix hurriedly as he rushed past.

Kit wasn't going to take Felix seriously until he entered the Great Hall.

The hall was buzzing with servants preparing for the feast. Kit's mother suggested that he rested as the party would be very late, so Kit went back to bed and slept till the afternoon.

That evening he dined with his uncle and made merry until late. Then he slept on a bed of straw, dreaming about tomorrow.

Kit King (10)
Calder House School, Colerne

A Day In The Life Of A Servant At Montacute House

At five o'clock in the morning I awoke and at once hurried upstairs to light the fire in the Great Hall. Then, I fetched my master's breakfast, carrying the heaviest tray you could imagine, I struggled down the stone stairs. Halfway up I put the tray down and looked out of the window. No one was coming up the drive! Sir Edward kept saying that Queen Elizabeth would arrive any time. When I reached the Great Hall, Sir Edward walked in in his black doublet. 'Where is Queen Elizabeth?' he asked.

'Not here, Sire,' I said.

Sir Edward sat down and clicked his fingers. I scurried over to him, carrying his breakfast. Then I ran down the twisting stairs to the kitchen.

When I entered the kitchen, everyone was running around. I helped heave a pig onto the table. It was very heavy and my friend Thomas put it on the spit. I had to turn the spit and make sure that the pig wasn't burnt on one side or raw on the other. It was hot, heavy work. After a while the spit boy arrived to take over.

Now it was my turn to return to the Great Hall with that pewter tray. It was so heavy! It seemed that I spent all day running up and down those stone stairs. Eventually, at ten o'clock I lit Sir Edward's fire and left the house and made myself comfortable on a bed of straw in the barn. At last I could sleep and enter a world with no work!

Benedict Skipper (10)
Calder House School, Colerne

A Day In The Life Of A Stable Boy At Montacute House

This morning I got up at dawn. I was given the privilege of grooming Sir Edward's horse. Meanwhile, Jones the head groom, was preparing four stables. When I had finished grooming Ebony, I saddled him, then I went to fetch seven other hunters.

By now it was 8 o'clock and I put them in the yard and returned to my duties. I normally have to groom and muck out Sir Edward's son's pony. By now I was hungry and some scraps arrived for my breakfast. I gobbled them up very fast.

Next I went to get the shire horses in. I was than ordered to help carry the luggage of my master's guests who had just arrived. By now it was 11 o'clock and some meat arrived on a trencher. I love trenchers because I can eat them! I had half an hour to eat my food but then it was back to work.

That afternoon, I had to ride to Yeovil with Jones to buy a hunter for Sir Edward's eldest son. I was allowed to go to look after the horses. It was a long ride to Yeovil. It took us an hour to choose the horse. He was called Kingsly. He was black with a white star. We paid for him and then set off. Two hours later we stopped at an inn in Brymton for the night. I stabled the horses and then went up into the loft, settled myself on some old sacks and fell fast asleep.

William Reynolds (10)
Calder House School, Colerne

A Day In The Life Of My Mum

First she wakes up in the morning when I go in to see her. She goes downstairs into the kitchen and makes a delicious breakfast. Then she takes my brother to school and me to Calder House. Then she drives away.

When she gets home she goes on the computer and does work for my dad. Later she has lunch, it smells lovely and tastes delicious. She works for another hour then plays tennis. Then she picks my brother and me up from school and takes us home.

When she gets home she goes into the kitchen and cooks us food. It is always fantastic. At nine o'clock she tells us to go to bed. Then she watches TV for five minutes and then she goes to sleep.

Harry Oliver (10)
Calder House School, Colerne

A Day In The Life Of My Brother, Thomas

Thomas wakes up at 7am. He goes to have a shower a soon as he wakes and then gets changed. He then gets in the car and goes to school. He doesn't like school! He is in Year 10 and is doing his GCSEs.

After school my mum picks Thomas and me up and takes us home. He has his tea and then goes to his piano lesson. He is very good on the piano. Then he goes to play golf. He has just become a member of the golf club where my mum works.

After he finishes playing golf he comes home and goes to bed.

Josh Walford (10)
Calder House School, Colerne

A Day In The Life Of My Dad

Every morning my dad, Paul, wakes up and gets dressed. Then he goes to Tesco to have a cooked breakfast.

Then he goes to the fish and chip shop. He has to cut the plaice to take the bones out. The shop smells of cooking oil and his clothes smell of frying and chicken. He goes to the shop at eleven in the morning and comes home at eleven at night.

When he gets home he washes and goes to have a drink of water. Then he goes to bed.

It's a hard job but he likes it.

Philip Robinson (10)
Calder House School, Colerne

Heights

Here I go! Look at those steps!
   'Alright Mum I'm coming.' I am doing this for Mum, she wants to see the view. Last step, I'll close my eyes.
   'Look,' says Mum
      I open my eyes. 'Aaarrrggghhh!' There's a long drop. I run straight down the steps. 'Phew I'm safe now!'

Alexandra Bearman (10)
Compton Dundon CE Primary School, Compton Dundon

A Day In The Life Of A Malteser

I want to get out of this packet and I can barely breathe. Every day I try to go to sleep but it's so humid I can't. The packet keeps on moving, I think there's someone outside. I feel like I am going to get eaten any minute now.

I am getting really tense. I have no hair, two eyes and I'm ugly. I don't know why anyone would want to eat me. Would you? I think I would taste disgusting! I am covered in sticky brown stuff but my insides feel really light. The packet is just opening and I feel my life has come to an end. My stomach is turning. Am I going to get eaten?

I think I am sat in the fridge. I can see cheese, milk, chocolate and fruit. Where am I? I think I am lost. The smell is disgusting. It smells of rotten eggs. It's horrible. I want to hold my nose but I haven't got one.

All of the bigger Maltesers are pushing towards the back of the packet. This had been going on for too long now. I declare war against the bigger Maltesers.

This went on for around three days and I was getting fed up. At last I can hear the words I have been waiting for - 'Can I have a packet of Maltesers please?'

Jenna Griffin (9)
Ferndale Junior School, Swindon

A Day In The Life Of Malteser, The Queen's Dog

I'm up already but she is not. I have to wait for her but I have to play, I can see a big orange ball. Sometimes I get breakfast myself but I get a nasty smack.

I am hungry as usual, I'm always hungry. I never sleep a wink because the Queen snores like a tractor and does not stop.

I decide I should get my breakfast myself for the biscuits are just left on the side. I get water from the sink and wash myself in the pot outside that the bins go in, I don't know why.

I can see the crown sitting there on the red chair, so I might just chew it like my old toy car!

Rebecca Ruddock (9)
Ferndale Junior School, Swindon

A Day In The Life Of A Ladybird

I have just woken up from my long sleep at home. I keep having to move out of the way of giant people, they have no respect for pretty ladybirds.

'Time for breakfast dear.'
'Yum breakfast. What is it?'
'Greenflies.'
'My favourite, yum. That was nice, thanks Mum.'
'You're welcome dear.'

I'm off to school now, school is fun, we get to learn facts and things about different insects. *Ring, ring,* school has started. Our teacher is Mrs Bottomly, she is called that because she has a big bottom.

'Now class, ladybird alphabet.'
'A, B, C, D, E, F, G, H, I, J . . .'
'Okay your homework today is to review the alphabet to your parents.'

Ding-dong! School has ended. Now I can play a game with my friends at the park. We huddle up and decide that we are going to play football with spider football web. After football we all go back to our cosy little homes.

Alexander Sanchez-Garcia (9)
Ferndale Junior School, Swindon

A Day In The Life Of A Dog

I've been lying here all night. I haven't slept a wink, she keeps snoring! I have been wondering when she is going to wake up so I can get my breakfast. I'm starving, I didn't get any tea last night.

I was bored of staying in the house on my own. She doesn't normally work all day. All I did was bark at the postman. Mind you, he was frightened. He jumped back from the door. I did think about eating the post but it is a bit chewy.

When she came home she had a nasty shock. I had ripped open my food bag and helped myself! It was delicious, but I did have a bad belly because I had eaten too much. She then put me outside in the rain.

It's cold out here. I promise I won't be naughty again Mum!

Abigail Nicholls (9)
Ferndale Junior School, Swindon

A Day In The Life Of A Malteser

I want to get out of this packet, I've been in here for so long but I can't breathe. I want to go to sleep in my packet but I am starting to melt. Now I have been put into the shop and oh my God, someone is picking me up.

That was a bumpy ride. I felt like I was on a roller coaster. I can finally breathe and see daylight once again but I am frightened because there are giants. I am nervous.

I roll out of my packet on into the backyard. The sun is so hot, Oh no I'm starting to melt! The giant has just picked me up. Oh my God, it's f-f-f-freezing in here but at least I'm not melting anymore.

Argh! Turn off the light. Where am I? All I can see is dairy stuff around me. Thank God I'm back in the warm.

I roll along outside the front door and onto the stony concrete (it hurts). I am covered in brown sticky stuff. Until I came out here I felt all light inside, now I'm all rocky and stony.

I wish I hadn't come out here now because there are lots more giants than I thought. Let me roll back inside. I think I'm safe once again.

Argh! Don't step on me you stupid ugly giant! Oh my God, a giant is picking me up. I'm right up against her face. Urgh! What is that smell? I want to hold my nose but I've just remembered, I haven't got one. My life is just about to end - *heeelp . . . !*

Charlotte Day (9)
Ferndale Junior School, Swindon

A Day In The Life Of My Appendix

I am in the body of . . . um . . . um . . . um . . . oh yes I am in the body of Samantha Telling. She hasn't got appendicitis yet although she has had a bad bellyache and has been sick quite a few times.

I don't feel so good. I'm getting a bit numb and I think I am getting extremely hot. Very, very hot. *Aaarrrggghhh!* That must have been bad for Sam up there.

Bang! Ooh stomach please save me. Kidney, lungs, heart, please, I don't want to go.

'What the heck is that?'

'Kidney, please save me!'

'Look, would you want to live in a jam jar all your life?'

'Ooh, I feel dead . . .'

Samantha Telling (8)
Ferndale Junior School, Swindon

A Day In The Life Of A Golden Eagle

I am waiting on a long branch. My prey is right in front of me. I swoop down and catch it. It's trying to get away but nothing can escape me.

I wait through the cold, windy night on the branch. I go for a fly around the mountains, Everybody hides from my deadly call. I go lower to the ground. Nobody is there. It is silent.

I go back to my branch and wait some more. Only a screech can be heard, but nothing else. I am going to the highest top on the tallest mountain to wait for a single sound but there is nothing.

I see something scuttling across the floor. I don't have the strength to move but I try to grab it. I just get it. I eat it bit by bit. My tummy is rumbling. I can't move, it feels like I've gone numb. I feel like I'm going to die. My babies are starving. There is nothing - not even a worm. My life is about to end.

Nathan Fry (8)
Ferndale Junior School, Swindon

A Day In The Life Of A Jelly Bean

Oh dear! I have been stuck in this jar for weeks and weeks. Ha! Ha! Someone's coming through that door, I can get out of this jar finally.

What about my friends? They'll probably come anyway but some of them might stay.

That lady is eating me, oh dear! Help! I am going down a long tube. It's disgusting, yuck!

What are they? They look like trees. What's that bright red pumping thing? What in the world is it? Oh dear I am going on a bumper ride but I cannot wait any longer.

Wow that was fun going down that slide. What . . . is . . . that? Oh no I'm in water, I'm getting flushed . . . !

Amie Hester (9)
Ferndale Junior School, Swindon

A Day In The Life Of The Queen's Dog

Ahhh, it's time to get up, I don't want to get up, it's Mum, she sets the alarm for 6am! Time for my breakfast, oh what am I having? I think it's chicken and gravy Chum! Yummy!

What! What's that, the door, oh no, time for my walk. Look there's Prince Harry, he's coming over, I like it when he comes over to me. I feel like I want to run free. If only Mum would let me off my lead to go see Harry.

What's she doing? She's letting me off my lead. I can finally run! Hooray! Oh but I will miss my chicken and gravy Chum from the palace. I think I will stay for the time being so I can eat more, then I will go.

Please can I be put back on my lead? I want to go home and sleep, but please don't bring Harry back, he will not let me go to sleep, he'll jump on me! Please don't bring him back I'll die! Thank God for that, he's gone home, I can go home now and have chicken and gravy Chum for my dinner and have a nice long sleep for about two hours!

Oh we're not going home yet we're going shopping. I hate going shopping it's boring!

She's buying chicken and gravy Chum for me! I think I might run away after dinner or should I stay here? I like it here it's nice. I'm not going to leave after all!

Lauren Haynes (9)
Ferndale Junior School, Swindon

A Day In The Life Of A Malteser

I've been in this packet, I don't really know how long. I wish somebody would eat me. I wish. I'm so chocolatey and crunchy. I'm chewy and so lovely. Yippee, someone's coming. They have picked me up. I'm out of the shop. I'm getting warmer and warmer, I can feel their breath. They have eaten me. Why have they tied me up to their tooth? She has got a tooth picker. No, that's not a tooth picker that's spit and a tongue!

Argh! She has spat me out. What are those creatures? Oh no they are ants, they're eating me.

I wish I had never been eaten in the first place.

Danyelle Morley (8)
Ferndale Junior School, Swindon

A Day In The Life Of Shawn Michaels

I was sitting in my locker room thinking about becoming the new World Heavyweight Champion when suddenly Eric Bichoff walked in and told me I had a match that night for the World Tag Team Championship. He asked me who I wanted my tag team partner to be. I said Edge.

He said, 'Alright then, the match is yours.'
Later on that night Edge wanted to speak to me.
I said, 'What do you want?'
'Next week you have a chance for the World Heavyweight Championship. All you have to do is sign this contract.'
I said, 'OK then, I will.'

I am very happy that I am getting a little shot at the World Heavyweight Championships. This is the greatest part of my life.

David Heskett (9)
Ferndale Junior School, Swindon

A Day In The Life Of A Malteser

I am still sitting in my packet. *I want to get out of here!* I've spent 4 days in this packet, maybe even longer. I am screaming, 'Let me out!' but no one can hear me.

Finally the time comes, I can hear the packet squeaking. I start singing for joy. My mates are upset with me. 'It's not fair, I really do want to live,' they shout.

I scream as I get picked out of the packet. Lauren is opening her large mouth and says, 'I am going to eat you.'

She does. I go in her horrible mouth and am wishing I hadn't. I pass out, her breath smells so bad I feel like being sick.

Her tongue is getting me soaked. I feel like it is raining but worse, like it is absolutely tipping down. It is as dark as anything. In the end we all get eaten.

Lauren Tyler (8)
Ferndale Junior School, Swindon

Euro 2004

I couldn't believe my eyes, it was over. My face was red, my body was hot and I was shaking with anger. I didn't know whether to cry or shout, I felt so disappointed. We had been knocked out of Euro 2004 because the referee had made a bad decision!

Jordan Phillips (10)
Highfield Primary School, Efford

Scared Of The Dark

Creak, crack tip-tap, bang! Shivering down my spine, a cold chill. Shivering from head to toe. Crying with fear. A floating sensation, wherever I stand. *Crash, bang,* something falls over. It's scary in the dark!

Kimberley Robinson (10)
Highfield Primary School, Efford

Dark

Standing in a dark room, lights flickering, seriously loud banging, light shadows with things coming out of nowhere. Creaking noises and footsteps coming closer. When the lights were turned on I looked down. It was not a ghost it was my cat. I wish I wasn't scared of the dark.

Natasha Cole (10)
Highfield Primary School, Efford

Planes

I was afraid, my stomach turned, my legs crumpled and I wanted to run in the other direction. I was so scared. Everyone was happy except me. The floor was moving, my life was over and when the plane took off, flying was the worst thing I'd ever done.

Tyler Williams (10)
Highfield Primary School, Efford

Crealy

I was excited but nervous all at the same time. I was hot and the palms of my hands became clammy. My body was shaking all over. There were so many sounds, people were shouting, laughing and screaming. A trip to Crealy is my favourite day out!

Curtis Munnings (10)
Highfield Primary School, Efford

Birth

Proud parents and relatives, the place smelled of disinfectant. I felt excited, cards being bought. The noise, the crying, it was very loud. Going home now, can't wait till next week. It's going to be a lot of fun around the house when the new baby comes home.

Kyla Bunker (10)
Highfield Primary School, Efford

Sleepovers

I am so excited but I also feel tired. I know I will not sleep tonight. I am normally scared of the dark but not tonight. I can't wait for it to get pitch-black. My friend is coming to my house for a sleepover and I can't wait!

Alexander Pearce (10)
Highfield Primary School, Efford

A Day In The Life Of Hillary Duff

It was dinner time. I was already having a terrible day. Danny Tailor accidentally pushed me. I fell over and ripped my brand new designer jeans. My mum would give me grief when I returned home.

I was right, she was so angry. I tried to explain it wasn't my fault, that Danny accidentally pushed me, but she wouldn't listen. She stomped upstairs and slammed my door!

That night I wished on a shooting star, for at least one day I could be someone famous. They seem to have it so much easier than us.

Next morning I awoke. Something was different. I wasn't in my own house. I staggered to the door. I saw my reflection in the mirror, but I didn't look like myself! I was the famous actress and singer, Hillary Duff.

I froze in astonishment. My wish had come true. I stood there for a moment, then rushed into the kitchen, to find a beautiful lady standing at the breakfast bar. She must have been my mum, I mean Hillary's mum.

'You're late for your photo shoot!' she said.

'Oh sorry.'

'Go and get ready then,' she replied. 'There's an outfit in your wardrobe.'

So without a fuss I zoomed to my room. I was still really tired and collapsed on the bed.

Someone started shaking me. I awoke with a fright. I was in my own house, Mum looking over me. 'Are you alright Caitlin?' she said.

'Yes fine, never better,' I replied happily.

Caitlin Mulroy (10)
Ladock CE Primary School, Truro

A Day In The Life Of . . .

It happens the same way every night, I got to bed, read then fall asleep into the deepest dreams. But this night was different.

Next morning thunder awoke me. I sprang out of bed and crept over to the window and peered out. It was diabolical, thudding rain, booming thunder and flashing lightning. I turned, there was a cracked mirror with a piece of glass missing. I stared into it. To my amazement I was Shane Richie. I retreated with a shriek and scanned the room with terror. I realised I wasn't in my house!

Quickly down the staircase I ran and found a tattered armchair. There was a note! 'If you want to go home you must do a good deed but you must do it alone!'

I was confused. I suddenly remembered about the cracked mirror in the bedroom. I rapidly ran upstairs, I found the mirror. This was my one and only chance to get home so I had to do it right.

I saw another note drift to the ground. 'You will find the missing piece of glass under a cushion. When the mirror is completed you will automatically return home'.

I sprinted down the stairs and to my surprise, there was a piece of glass protruding from under the cushion. I tugged it, entered the bedroom where the mirror hung. With two deep breaths I carefully placed the glass into the mirror. Frozen, a ray of light overtook my body and within seconds I was at home in *my* comfortable bed.

Rebecca Trethewey & Thai Batchelor (11)
Ladock CE Primary School, Truro

A Day In The Life Of A Frog

Have you ever heard of a watch? Well I think it's called that. I call it a timeteller.

It was raining.

'We must protect the timeteller,' bellowed Seymour, another frog.

Why? I thought. It should like water like us frogs, but I made no complaints. I mean why should I? I lived in a deep pond, not much pondweed for dirt to attach to, and a large waterfall in the corner.

It didn't take me and Seymour long to cover the timeteller. I didn't need the timeteller to know if it was morning or evening. I settled down on a rock. I tried to keep my eyes open, but it was no use. When I awoke the sun was high in the sky.

I tried to get off the rock but my feet seemed welded. I called out, 'Seymour.'

'Coming,' came a muffled voice. When he saw me he jumped into the waterfall. The water from the waterfall hit me. I was free.

'I'm stuck in some pondweed,' came a voice.

I dived under the waterfall and saw Seymour. He was stuck in a giant strand of pondweed. His back legs were dangling uselessly. I had never been behind the waterfall before.

'Hurry up,' called Seymour. With one push, Seymour was free.

We looked around. It was cool, enormous and dark. A perfect place. It had been an exciting day I thought as I settled down to sleep.

Alex Piper (9)
Ladock CE Primary School, Truro

A Day In The Life Of My Hamsters, Bubble And Squeak

I awoke this morning next to my friend Squeaker. We had been awoken by Emily stirring in bed. I opened my eyes, I could see her getting out. I had been planning, planning to escape! I squeaked loudly to say good morning, Squeaker squeaked as well. I saw Emily walk past our cage. I could just see her get her nightgown on, I guess she was going downstairs. Now was my chance to escape.

I squeezed through the bars and fell onto the carpet and scuttled under her cabinet. After a few minutes she was back. I saw her come over to our cage. I could just hear her muttering, 'Great, just great!'

I heard her walk over to the door, she closed it.

There was complete silence. I slowly made my way out from under her cabinet. Suddenly a large hand reached for me, I ran as fast as I could. Then everything went black. Then I realised that Emily had her hand over me, she picked me up very gently, then she placed me back in my cage. I let out a loud squeak as if to say, 'Squeak I'm back.'

Then I heard some scrambling down the tube. Then I went to find some food and our water bottle. I heard Emily get back into bed. Then I went back to my bed of cotton wool and I slept for the rest of the day. Well, what an adventure I had today. Goodbye readers!

Emily Richards (10)
Ladock CE Primary School, Truro

A Day In The Life Of Colin The Vet

One very dark morning a vet called Colin was walking to work when he accidentally stood in a bucket of paint. Colin attempted to get it off. He stood in pavement cracks, went under a ladder and tripped over a black cat.

Finally he removed it and just realised what he had done. *Bad luck is stalking me,* he thought.

When Colin arrived at work his first patient was a rat. The rat was ill and in pain so he had to put it down. The second patient was a bat. The bat had a broken wing so it had to be bandaged, then the owner departed until it was time to collect the bat at the end of the day.

Colin was still thinking about bad luck. His next patient was a Brazilian constrictor. Suddenly the anaconda squeezed the vet, crushing him tightly and swallowed him *whole!* There was a high-pitched scream! The owner was terrified. A cat turned to the bat and said, 'Not his day, is it?'

In the end the snake was put down. Let this be a lesson. *There is such a thing as bad luck, so beware!*

Joseph Moore (11)
Ladock CE Primary School, Truro

A Day In The Life Of A Dragon
(Inspired by 'The Wee Free Men' and 'A Hat Full of Sky' by Terry Pratchett)

For those of you who do not know Nac Macfeegles are pixdacies. They are six inches tall, similar to fairies, but they are especially dangerous when drinking beer and famous for fighting and stealing. If you ever want to see one, if you are brave enough, put a bottle of rum outside your window and wait!

I was sitting, on a misty morning, outside my cave on the side of Dragon Cliff, overlooking the sea. It was breakfast time and I was enjoying my breakfast of tasty humans. Suddenly, with a swoop, a buzzard came from the sky and dropped a Nac Macfeegle at my feet. It was Hamish, the Great Nac Macfeegles aviator. Hamish told me that the fairies were burning all the pubs and had started fights with the Nac Macfeegles and other dragons. I was very angry and set off in a rage to destroy the fairies.

We finally found the evil fairies. They had burnt my favourite pub. I took hold of some fairies and squeezed. Their heads fell off, magically new heads appeared but these were evil heads. Sharp, pointy ears, fang-like teeth that could peck like chickens, pale skin and evil black eyes, ready to blind their victims. Blood flew around me as fairies and pixdacies fought a fierce battle. I discovered a secret store of beer. Picking up a barrel I crept away, heading back to my cave. I sat down and drank from the barrel, the cold beer slid down my throat. . .

Steven Pinkerton (10)
Ladock CE Primary School, Truro

A Day In The Life Of The Mac Nacfeegles
(Inspired by 'The Wee Free Men' by Terry Pratchett)

Have you heard of the Mac Nacfeegles? Well we are six inches tall and we like drinking, stealing and fighting.

It was dark. We were in a hole. We were going to invade the officer's house. Well, he was in the shower.

'One of you lock the bathroom door, the rest destroy anything and vandalise the chandelier.'

The three wee men took out their swords and chopped the table into hundreds and hundreds of bits. The Mac Nacfeegles unlocked the bathroom door and ran down a rabbit hole that was actually a secret Mac Nacfeegle base. The officer ran out of the bathroom and saw the vandalism caused by the three wee men.

Down in the rabbit hole the Mac Nacfeegles were investigating the stolen goods. One of the drunken three wee men took out a sword and waved it at the officer. The feegle stabbed his sword into the officer's shoe. Feegle and the officers had wars from that day on.

Ben Palmer (10)
Ladock CE Primary School, Truro

A Day In The Life Of A Demon

Once a demon called Nightmare lived in a volcano. He was awakened by two armies, one red and one blue. I was falling into Nightmare's body.

Suddenly I stopped, opened my eyes and looked around. I just found out who I was, the demon from the volcano. I had been transformed. My giant arm picked up my sword and put on my armour. I was ready for battle!

My sword was as heavy as an elephant's body. My arm was as big as a human body with legs. There in front of me was the king, the leader of the red and blue armies. He was a samurai, with black, curly hair which was long. One of his guards stood in front of him, protecting him. He had the one sword I feared, the *sword of light!*

Suddenly, a crack in the ground appeared and swallowed me whole! Skeleton bones appeared in the lava as I fell.

They disappeared in the darkness. Sped over the normal limits. I travelled down and down and down to the ground and *thump!* I was unconscious.

I opened my eyes to see I was transformed into a human form, my own body. I thought to myself, *that was a lucky escape from an unlucky quest.*

Michael Shawcross (11)
Ladock CE Primary School, Truro

Stage Academy

My hands were sweating. The music started playing. I started dancing. I was scared. I started to sing. My friend started to sing too. I was very sweaty. My heart was pounding. The music stopped. We finished. The next band was up. I waited for the results. I won!

Hannah Mead (9)
Marldon CE Primary School, Marldon

Running A Race

It was the beginning of the race and I was racing against the fastest person in the school. I heard the whistle. I was running as fast as I could. My heart was pounding, I was losing my breath. As I was near the end, it happened. I had lost.

Emma Singleton (8)
Marldon CE Primary School, Marldon

The Wheel

I was going on a big wheel. My tummy was pounding. In a minute I was in the seat. Next I was going pale as I went up high. Spinning through the air made me go sweaty like I was going to be sick. The ride was ending. I survived the ride.

How?

Courtenay Clarke (8)
Marldon CE Primary School, Marldon

Mini Saga

Can I do it? It looks very dangerous, but I will give it a try. Here I go, *Argh!* My heart is pounding. I'm not sure I will be safe and sound. But now I've arrived at the bottom of the death slide. What a fab day I have had.

Frankie Dryden (9)
Marldon CE Primary School, Marldon

Mission Space

When I went to Florida I went on a ride called Mission Space. It was great! My mum and brother did not want to. I went round and round, I felt sick. I held it until the end of the ride. Then oooh . . . sick . . . as a parrot!

Kalam Uddin (8)
Marldon CE Primary School, Marldon

Seasons

I shiver as a trickle of snow runs down my back. I knew it. It had to come, the coldness of winter has evolved from the leaves of autumn. Next it will be the warm spring. Then will come the flowers of summer, which have emerged from the buds of spring.

Bryony Parris (8)
Marldon CE Primary School, Marldon

Spooky Ride

I never said I wanted to go in this spooky ride with my brother. We are ready to go! My brother's excited, I'm all glum.

'Fasten your seat belts.'

'We're off!'

We rushed through the ride like a roller coaster. I was impressed - I thought it would be slower!

Robyn Engstrom (8)
Marldon CE Primary School, Marldon

My Holiday

My name is Spikeless the albino ferret. During the summer holidays, my owner went to Wales so me and my friends (five of them), went to stay with the Dyne family at Hill Barton. It was really great there because every day we were put in a big stable with lots of pipes, tubes, tyres and much more to climb on. We would all go mad and get bushy-tailed and very bouncy, romping around and having play fights.

Sometimes I was naughty a bit and I bit Sam's ear (Sam looked after me). He squealed in pain but he still liked me. Sam's mum cleaned out our hutches every day and she fed us extra eggs. I hope we go there next year.

Sam Dyne (11)
Morchard Bishop CE Primary School, Morchard Bishop

A Day In The Life Of David Beckham

It was in the sunny, posh part of Madrid. David Beckham was lying in his boxers half asleep.

'David, David wake up, it's nearly time for training with Real Madrid.'

'Oh no!' yelled David as he flung the covers over him. 'The first day back in the summer training and I'm going to miss it.'

'No you're not, don't worry, I've got your training kit out and your new silver boots.'

So he got up and put on his shirt with the glazing badge looking at him and his shorts, socks and boots. 'Right, I'm ready.' And was out of the door before Victoria's eyes blinked. David got into his brand new Bentley and raced off.

Meanwhile at the training ground everyone was waiting for him.

'Maybe he's ill,' suggested Roberto Carlos.

'No, he would have phoned,' said another.

Finally he had arrived to find everyone had started.

Then David looked at his watch and realised he was half an hour late.

The manager noticed David and called him over. *Uh-oh,* David thought to himself, *this doesn't look good.*

David jogged over. 'Sorry boss, I got stuck in a traffic jam for 15 minutes.'

'Sorry David,' said the manager, 'that isn't good enough.'

'But boss!'

'That was your last warning David, and you've blown it. You're a very talented player and I don't want to have to let you go, but I have to get rid of you.'

'Please, I'll do anything.'

'I said *no!*'

Loren Eginton (11)
Morchard Bishop CE Primary School, Morchard Bishop

TV

I slid down the polished wooden banister and flew over the blue carpet onto the comfy sofa. I picked up the remote control and pressed the rubbery channel 1 button. My square eyes went fuzzy, this could only mean I had entered the magical world of TV!

Emma Sparrow (11)
Morchard Bishop CE Primary School, Morchard Bishop

My Birthday!

I ran up the shimmering stairs as fast as my legs could carry me. I jumped on the soft bed and shouted at sleepy Mum and Dad. 'It's my birthday!'

I dragged Mum and Dad downstairs grabbing a huge present on my way while ripping it into tiny pieces.

Jessica Kate Powell (11)
Morchard Bishop CE Primary School, Morchard Bishop

A Day In The Life Of Neil Armstrong

I suddenly felt nervous as I put on my suit and prepared: I proudly strode into Apollo 11 and set myself up ready for launching. The countdown began, 5 . . . 4 . . . 3 . . . 2 . . . 1 . . . We were off and the noise - well that was just terrific! I quickly started to tinker with the wicked gismo of the rocket, it was soon under my control. We fired ourselves into 1st position. The rocket sped up as we made ourselves comfortable. By now we had got used to hovering above the flooring and began to feel a great deal more relaxed about what was going to happen next.

The moon was already faintly in view; I briskly floated over to the control panel unit to put us in a good position for landing on the moon. I was the first one to step on the moon, it was wonderful. I felt I was the happiest man in the universe! It was obvious that this was the most fantastic day of my life. Buzz came rushing out to share the excitement with me. We called Ground Control to tell them what had happened; it seemed like they were over the moon as well!

Then I said these few words; *'That's one small step for man. One giant leap for mankind.'*

Alex Porter (9)
Newton St Cyres Primary School, Exeter

A Day In The Life Of Linda Barker

'Wake up, wake up!' My husband was calling me, all I could hear was a light echo drumming in my head. 'Wake up, wake up!'

I slowly rose like a robot recovering from its cut-out engine. I peeled back my sleeping mask, the sun was peeping through the gap in the cream curtains. I felt too fragile to be painting today so I reached out for the phone and started to dial my client's number, when I remembered that today I was meant to be filming for 'Changing Rooms'. I fell back on the pillow in laziness.

I grabbed my bag from the stool in the kitchen and set off for filming.

As soon as I got there they showed me the room. I fainted in shock, I had never seen a room like it. I felt like I was in a time warp, it was so sixties. There was brown flowery wallpaper with a brown carpet and a dingy green sofa and two chairs. I don't know how people lived in it!

Later when I had recovered from my big shock, I set to work making interiors, cushions and curtains, and what I do best, annoying Handy Andy!

I arrived back at my house at 8.30pm, collapsed on the leather sofa and soon I fell asleep. The brown sixties room arrived back in my head.

Megan Kingdom-Davies (10)
Newton St Cyres Primary School, Exeter

Joan Of Arc - Diary Extract

Morning

It's the middle of a raging war in France. But the king still does nothing! He hasn't even been crowned. I mean even *I* could stop this war if I wanted to. I could write and complain. I'm going to think about it seriously. I'm going out for a walk now. I'm going down to the Fairy Oak. I wonder if my mysterious voices will start whispering again. For a long time the voices have been telling me to help the rightful king. Whatever am I supposed to do? I mean I'm only 11 and this is serious war! I might be able to help him. A bit. I'll be glad if he comes to the throne. It will be partly my work.

Afternoon

I was down at the Fairy Oak a while ago. The voices were there. They were saying the same thing. I think I'll go and help the king. The voices must be serious if they continually pester me for ages! Well, if I'm going to make France a better place I'd better get ready. I must find a way to tell the king without a disaster. That's going to be hard. I mean - the king's a coward! I'd better start thinking. I reckon that if anyone is ever remembered who was in this war, I think it will probably be me. Some people might think I'm idle. But I'm not. I'm just going to do something brilliant. Something worth remembering.

Lucy Harrison-Prentice (9)
Newton St Cyres Primary School, Exeter

A Day In The Life Of Queen Elizabeth I

I woke slowly and looked up at the canopy of my four-poster bed, then I remembered this was to be the day that Mary Queen of Scots was beheaded. I gracefully got out of bed and wandered over to my mirror and stared into it. My small, pale complexion stared back, I went over to my bells and rang for my maids to dress me. They brought in my black mourning dress and started to dress me.

When my maids had finished getting me ready, I went outside to my royal carriage which was to take me to the beheading. We drew up to the royal viewing stand and I was helped out of the carriage. There was chattering all around and then suddenly there was silence as Mary walked out onto the scaffold.

I could not watch, though I heard the swish of the blade through her neck. I turned round just in time to see Mary's head roll off the chopping block. I sat down sharply, buried my head in my hands and wept. The executioner then picked up Mary's head and stuck it on a stake and showed it to the crowd, as a sign of what happens when you commit treason. People were pushing through towards the scaffold with handkerchiefs trying to collect blood. It is said that the blood of a beheading will heal you of blemishes.

Later on I went by myself to pay my respects to Mary. When I got back to the castle, I went straight to bed and as soon as my head touched the pillow, I fell asleep.

Natasha Richards (10)
Newton St Cyres Primary School, Exeter

A Day In The Life Of Lindsay Lohan

As I got up the telephone was ringing, I rushed towards it. As I got to the ringing phone, it went on to the answer machine. I listened to the message it was Mark Waters, the top film director. He said that he had a job for me as the lead role in 'Mean Girls' with other actors such as Rachel McAdams, Tim Meadows, Andy Poehler, Ana Gasteyer and Tina Fey. He left his number for me to ring him back to find out my wage and all of the facts for the film.

When I got off the phone I started yelling, 'I will earn £1,000,000 just for playing the lead role in Mean Girls!'

I ran into my mum's room still in my pyjamas, I yelled my wonderful news at her. All she could say was, 'That's amazing dear.' She also said happy birthday to me and then I remembered that today was my birthday. She gave me a picture of Jamie Lee Curtis and me, as she was a good friend when we were filming 'Freaky Friday'.

We went out and had lunch in a five star Chinese restaurant. I made sure that I didn't eat any fortune cookies.

When I was getting ready for my party. There was a knock at the door, it was a man.

He said, 'Are you ready? I would like to give you a ride in my purple limo.'

I was rushed off to my disco party

I woke up and looked round . . . where was I?

Charley Finch (10)
Newton St Cyres Primary School, Exeter

A Day In The Life Of A German Spy

I was soaring through the air carrying four bombs on my aeroplane to bomb England with. Suddenly I was shot at by the British army. They hit my right wing causing me to spin round and eventually to crash.

When I crashed I collided with a tree. The people on the farm saw me crash so they came running out to see what had happened. I tried to get away but they saw me crawling along the floor. I tried to speak in English, but I couldn't. They had guns so they surrounded me, then they called the armed forces and they held me captive in the cellar.

After a little while, some soldiers came to collect me. They took me away in handcuffs and chains. I went to prison that day and they put me through hard labour until I started to sweat. I wondered what was to become of me, would I ever get out of here alive? Would I ever see my family again?

It was a cold and lonely night as I stayed awake, worrying what the future was to bring . . .

Nathan Jackson (10)
Newton St Cyres Primary School, Exeter

Angelina Ballerina

As I woke up in the early morning, all pictures surround me of my friends and me. My mother came in and said good morning to me. Then I got up and practised for my big day ahead of me. I put on my warming-up tutu and practised all my five positions. 1st, 2nd, 3rd, 4th and 5th.

My mother called me for breakfast so I went downstairs and had some jam on toast. The jam was yummy and the toast was crunchy and all the food was in my tummy.

Afterwards I put on my cooking tutu and made a cake for my ballet teacher. She was kind most of the time but when we were naughty, she wouldn't be happy.

She gave us a step that I couldn't do, so I cried and cried.

On the stage I was frightened, all the other littler dancers were skipping round and I was on my own. The step I was taught, I remembered I couldn't do it. I tried before the curtains opened and for once I did it. I tried again and again. I did it! I did it and then I did it again. The curtains opened and I wasn't worried.

At the end I said to myself, 'I did it!'

I went home to my bed and all night long I was dreaming of how good I was.

Jennie Cocker (9)
Newton St Cyres Primary School, Exeter

The Cave Troll

I was living in a cave when *bang! Bang!* Something or someone was bashing my door.
   'Open Cave Troll.'
   'Go away!' I said feeling tired and ill. 'I'm sick.'
   'I've got you a present?'
   'Mmm . . . ?' I said confused.
   'A present,' Sam said.
   I opened the door, next thing I knew I was tied up and thrown into the dungeons of castle Camelot. I was sad and ill; I think I had an infected tummy.
   It was night-time, in other words bedtime. Guards were guarding me, I could have easily killed them but my tummy hurt so much I couldn't do anything but lie there until the morning.

The next day I woke up feeling as right as rain but two of the guards were still by the door, so I just pushed them out of the way, they were not a problem.
   I pushed past everybody else and legged it, I was nearly out of the castle when, 'Stop right there!' It was Sam.
   'Get lost!' I said.
   'No, you shall die!' Sam screamed.
   'Oh yeah!' And with that I sat on his head.
   I ran out of the castle but suddenly I felt ill again, my tummy was killing me, I couldn't shout for help, if I did all the knights of Camelot would hear me and I'd be put in prison again, so I crawled on. When I reached my door, I was safe and I never opened that door again.

Edward Leyland-Simpson (9)
Newton St Cyres Primary School, Exeter

Slipping Away

As the old Viking lay on his deathbed thinking about his last adventure. He could hear the cries of his men and screams from his enemies and he could see them falling to their knees, as he slowly slipped away, he could see his ship drawing near to take him home . . .

Luke Hodgin (11)
Pauntley CE Primary School, Newent

A Day In The Life Of Tigers

Hunting down meat, searching through dark forbidden forests. My teeth covered with delicious red blood. Silence - I heard strange sounds but no sign of anything. Then I saw lots of people, I counted them all. '12, just about room.'
    I ran up and . . . Gone!
    'All finished,' I growled.

Jordan Louise Morrow (8)
St John's CE Primary School, Cheltenham

A Day In The Life Of A Planet

While I was awake, I was spinning so fast I couldn't even see. The stars were like a blur of light. I looked in front of my eyes, it was bare. Suddenly I saw an unusual metal shape, it had flames from its behind. *What could it be?* I thought.

Aston Robinson (8)
St John's CE Primary School, Cheltenham

A Day In The Life Of A Cat

I was just relaxing on the couch when I was picked up and put into my cage. I was taken by car to the vets. I was so scared at first but as usual I was given some milk. While I was drinking it, they injected me. Zzzz!

Francesca Wallbank (8)
St John's CE Primary School, Cheltenham

A Day In The Life Of A Baby!

I was in a wee cot when I woke up in the morning, just then the door slammed. A whole group of people were crowding me.
  'What a cute baby,' someone whispered.
  A baby, I thought. *So that's what I am.*
  My mum said, 'This is Kerry, our cute darling.'

Kerry Palmer-Hadfield (8)
St John's CE Primary School, Cheltenham

A Day In The Life Of An Evacuee

The ice-cold teardrops were running down my cheeks. It wasn't pleasant waving goodbye to my mum from the train. She said that I was going on holiday but I realised I wasn't. I looked at a little boy opposite, who reminded me of Dad. Will I ever see him again?

Charlotte Morris (8)
St John's CE Primary School, Cheltenham

A Day In The Life Of A Baby

'*Waa! Waa!* I want my food. Mum hurry up! Hey, that's my toy. Hey, put me down I want to stay here. I'll start crying even more!

Waa! That's more like it, Dad gave me my bottle. I didn't know it was this hard being a baby - *help me now!*'

Ella Hargreaves (7)
St John's CE Primary School, Cheltenham

A Day In The Life Of The Young Pilot

'Camp at last.'
  Jonnie has been crying all the way here, he hasn't learned how to control his feelings . . .

An hour later . . .
  'Am I still asleep? What's happening?'
  'Jonnie, Jonnie! Where are you?'
  'Come on old friend, the siren's going, we've been attacked and you've got to get the planes in the sky before they're bombed.'
  'Hurry! War has started.'

We've been flying for two days and I don't know where Jonnie is, I hope he's alright. I look behind me, all I can see is smoke and ashes. I can't help thinking of all those who have died in the war. Will it be me who goes down soon? I don't know . . . ?

The next day I was shot down, I plummeted towards the ground. I awoke with a bright light shining into my numb eyes. I think I can recall being told that Jonnie was dead. I would have cried but I can't. I don't feel sadness for I am a *ghost* stuck between worlds, telling a tale.

Claire Brooks (10)
St Mewan CP School, St Austell

A Day In The Life Of A Football Stadium

It's the day before the football match and everybody is getting ready for the big day. The groundsmen are mowing and painting the lines on the pitch. They also need to make sure that the lights are on inside the stadium.

'This one needs changing,' says Bob.

It's match day and the crowd is starting to fill up.

'One ticket for today's match,' says Ed.

The staff are getting instructions that if anybody causes trouble, they will be asked to leave.

The people in the Sky box are also getting ready for the game. The cameraman sets the camera up so that people can watch the game on TV.

The teams come out.

'Go Frankie!' says a boy in the crowd.

It's half-time and Ed has gone to the snack bar. 'A can of pop and some doughnuts please,' says Ed.

It's the last minute of the game, but what is this? He shoots and the crowd are roaring, but the goalie has saved it. It's the end of the game and the crowd clap the players off the pitch.

George Hyde-Linaker
St Mewan CP School, St Austell

A Day In The Life Of My Cat

It's 1am. I'm not tired because I usually sleep during the day. My owners come and wake me up though. I lie on my back and they tickle my tummy. I go back to sleep after that. It's now 1.30am and one of my owners, Jack can't sleep, he's thinking of scorpions under his bed.

2.15am. Jack has just gone into my adult owner's room. I stay on Jack's bed all night, thinking he might come back. He doesn't. I'm upset that he hasn't come back.

When I saw him in the late morning, I saw he had calmed down. I was lucky it was Saturday so I could stay with him all day. But they went out. Me and my brother guard the house when they're out. I sit at the front door, my brother sits at the back door. Usually, a rival cat comes along and it ends up with us having a fight.

Jack came back really chuffed and he had a keyring. He'd been to Flambards. On the keyring he had his hands off the handlebars on the Hornetcoaster. That was the end of my day.

Jack Tucker (10)
St Mewan CP School, St Austell

A Day In The Life Of Rupert

Oh no, it's Saturday that means Natalie. Oh well I might as well look on the bright side. I will get lots of apples and carrots. Oh look, here she comes now. 'Hi Natalie, have you got something to eat?'
    'Oh get off Rupert, let me get you a carrot.'
    'Oh yummy. Oh no, not the fly spray!'
    'Rupert, it's not going to hurt you!'
    'How do you know?'
    'Fine, you win, let me get the hoof pick.'
    'Mind the frog Natalie.'
    'I will.'

'There, good boy, let me get you a carrot.'
    'How about an apple?'
    'Or an apple!'
    'Yum!'
    'Now Rupert, let me do your mane and tail.'
    'Okay Nat.'
    'Good boy Rupert, now all that's left is your body.'
    'Then can I have my lunch?'
    'Then you can have your lunch!'
    'Thank you, Nat.'
    'Rupert, you're the best pony in the world.'
    'Gee, thanks.'

Natalie Keveth (10)
St Mewan CP School, St Austell

A Day In The Life Of A Fish

One day I was swimming around my fish tank. Suddenly Flo came up to me.

'Hi Bubbles.'
'Hi Flo,' I said, scared stiff.
'What's the matter?' she said.
'Er nothing,' I said again.
'Well alright then but I do think something's wrong.' And she swam off.

When she was gone I slowly began to cry so I went back home and dozed off. I awoke with a bang on my door. I guessed it was Flo back again to see if I was alright. I opened the door and immediately said, 'I'm fine.'

'Excuse me!' said someone.
I opened my eyes.
'I'm here to see, erm, who is it?' said the voice again. 'A Mr Bibbles, no Bubbles, sorry!'
'What do you want?' I said.
'I'm a sales manager, I've come to sell your tank.'

Flo, she'd set me up. That's why she'd asked me was I okay! So I told the manager I was going out and wasn't selling my house. So I went to Flo's house and she admitted she'd set me up.

What a day I've had!

Bethany Scoble (10)
St Mewan CP School, St Austell

A Day In The Life Of Lady Jane Grey

It was a week and two days when it happened . . . when Edward died. I didn't even want to be crowned queen . . . it was all my father's idea really. He said it was better to keep the Protestant rulers ruling.

I know Mary's against me being queen and I know Mary should have been crowned instead of me

I keep having these nightmares, horrible nightmares, of my head on the block . . . the axe a metre before my head and then . . . then I wake up and realise that it's only four hours until it really happens!

Emily Bell (10)
St Mewan CP School, St Austell

A Day In The Life Of Hector

Hello, I'm Hector. Each day I go in my field for three hours and I poop nine times. When I go out on rides I get bored because this girl Olivia can't go on the road yet, because I'm too big. So I start playing up. First I canter when Olivia wants me to trot. I trot when she wants me to canter then I start being plain stubborn, I'm a big pain! Olivia hasn't fallen off me yet but she will do, some day!

Oh yes, each time I'm doing a nice trot or canter I need a big plop, there goes my appetite on the floor, a big poo not to mention I'm 17.3hh!

Hee, hee, ha, ha, ha because I'm so big and Olivia is so small, she looks like an ant. Because I'm a boy and the other horses that I live with, they're big girls. Each day in the field, they corner me and kick, and bite, rear and buck me on purpose. They're stubborn things and it is every day that they bully me like that! At least Olivia rides me. I am really a little angel!

Olivia Grose (9)
St Mewan CP School, St Austell

A Day In The Life Of A Bloodcell

'Cancer has hit my body and it is time to prove myself. I must save the lungs.'

The battle . . .
   Message to brain, 'We're hit!'
   'See the doctor. I'll fight it.'
   'I'm at front base now. I must find General White. Hello General, can you arm me with the latest nicotine pouch 35617 please? Thank you!'

'Forward march. What's that? It looks like a lung cancer pill.'
   'Lung cancer pill 3188 at your service.'
   'Troops dispatch. Come with me to the lungs 3188, I need your help.'
   'Sweet mother of me, what has happened here?' I'm thinking aloud as I look at the blackened lungs. 'Fire at will,' I'm saying as their nicotine troops charge to attack.
   'Aargh, eee, aaa!' The nicotine screams.
   What? I'm thinking as I'm dragged away by someone I can't see.
   'Tell us why you attacked,' someone was saying as I woke.
   'Never!' I shouted. That was a mistake because I felt a whip hit me. 'No!' I was whipped another three times.
   'Stop!' someone was shouting.
   Then I heard fighting, lots of it. A person I couldn't see was setting me free. '3188!'
   'Yes!'
   'Thank you.'
   'Don't thank me yet, we have still got to clear the lungs.'
   So we set off shooting the nicotine to the floor until the lungs were completely cleared.

'All clear General White,'
   'Well done.'
   'Thank you. Oh and I wish to keep 3188 as a friend instead of letting him go down the waste tunnel.'
   'Very well.'
   'Thank you again.'

Patrick Nichols (10)
St Mewan CP School, St Austell

A Day In The Life Of A Turtle

'Hi Jellyfish, how are you today? I'm great thanks!'

14th March 9904 - under the water.

It was a great day under the water because it was my birthday. It was my second birthday and I was so excited. My mum had bought me one big present. At 11am I opened my big present, it was excellent. 'I've always wanted one of these,' I said to my mum.

'Well that's good then,' I remember her soft voice saying.

Two days later I remember trying out my big underwater UFO, it was fabulous. I can just remember the three purple buttons that said 'go', 'stop' and 'drive'.

The next day I remember going to see my friends Jellyfish, Octopus, Shark and Fishy Fish. Fishy Fish tried out the UFO first then Octopus, then Jellyfish and last of all Shark. They all thought it was fantastic.

I remember me saying that I was tired and that I'd better go home to bed. So off I went in my new UFO. When I got home I had a glass of milk and then went to bed very happily. I was very grateful for everything I had.

Robyn Parkin-Jones (10)
St Mewan CP School, St Austell

The Cave

Once upon a time there was a girl called Meme and her five best friends. They were called Mat, Ash, Emily, Adam and Kelly. They were very cool.

One day they went out for a walk and they came across a bridge made out of wood. Meme said, 'Come on everybody let's cross it.'
They said, 'Okay then' but Mat said 'No!'
Meme said, 'Why not?'
'Because I am - I am scared.'
'Come on Mat, I will help you across,' said Meme.
'Okay then,' Mat said.
So carefully they walked across the bridge. The bridge was so old and as they walked across it, it made large creaking sounds. They were scared that it was going to break. They were glad to get to the other side.
They carried on walking until they all got to a cave. When they got there Emily said, 'You love Mat, you love Mat!' to Meme.
'No I don't, I love Adam,' replied Meme.
'You love Mat!' teased Emily.
Meme got very upset and said, 'Go away!'
So they did.
Meme stayed there for the night and she got very cold and scared and started to cry. She decided to cheer herself up and started singing.

The next day her friends came back. Emily said sorry to Meme. Meme replied, 'You'd better be.' Giving each other a big hug.
'Come home and we'll have a party,' said Emily.
So they walked home together and when they got there Emily got Adam to come to the party as a surprise for Meme.
Meme was really happy to be home again with her family, friends and Adam.

Jessica Bowditch (10)
Tatworth Primary School, Tatworth

The Screaming Skull

One day a little boy named Robbie was walking through the quarry. In the quarry was an old rusted caravan, it had boarded-up windows with aluminium and had graffiti all over it.

He touched the caravan to look in the crack in a piece of aluminium. Suddenly the lock fell off. From inside, a brick was thrown and knocked off a piece of aluminium. A body was thrown out afterwards and a ghost came out as well.

Robbie was so spooked, he nearly died. Something came over him and unexpectedly he grabbed a rock and threw it right in the ghost's mouth!

All of a sudden, Robbie heard a high-pitched, faint scream. He poked his head around the door. His eardrums were so numb, it was a skull on fire with a rat crawling in its eye sockets. It had bright red blood oozing out of its other socket and green slime all over it. Robbie couldn't stop staring at it, he wanted to peg it. Robbie thought nothing could possibly get worse but it was just starting.

He thought he shouldn't tell anyone but the next day he told the police. At first they didn't believe him but when they went to the caravan in the quarry and saw the body they said sorry to Robbie for not believing him.

The police broke the skull in half and thought everything would be okay but that night a small grey cloud landed on Robbie's bed. A flash of lightning filled the room and he saw the skull once again. Another flash of lightning filled the room and set it on fire. Robbie felt a pain that night which went on for the rest of his life.

Every Saturday, if it's a full moon, you will hear screaming, it will haunt your dreams!

Harry Ingrams & Kyran Parsons (10)
Tatworth Primary School, Tatworth

Spiders

One miserable day on the outskirts of Somerset, there lived a cramped family in a small house. The small house was in Hillside Lane right on the end of the street. You could never miss my house, it's the smallest of the lot.

In my house there lives my mum Sophie, she's got blonde curly hair and she loves her art. She never stops drawing. Hey, let's carry on, we could go on forever. Also I've got a dad called William, he's got black hair and he loves football. I've also got a little brother called Jeremy. He's got blond hair too and you've guessed it, he loves Power Rangers, dinosaurs, transformers, the lot. Hey I forgot me - George.

It suddenly went pitch-black, I tried to find the light, I finally found it and I opened one eye but saw nothing. I opened the other eye, I shouted, 'Help, help, help!' Right in front of me was a six foot high giant *spider!* I ran over to the window, there were spiders invading the city. Luckily there was a shotgun on the table, I took one shot, *bang! Splat!* Green goo everywhere. Phew, the spider was dead. I looked out of the window again, they were webbing people up and killing them. I had to do something, I thought for a sec, 'Oh damn, my mum is on a date with my dad, I'll just have to fight them alone!'

To be continued . . .

George Bragg (10)
Tatworth Primary School, Tatworth

The Adventure

As Rafiki lifted the young lion cub Kiara to the sun the animals of Pride Rock bowed in honour to their new princess. She grew big and strong.

It was dawn and Kiara went out for an adventure. She sat on a rock looking far out into the outlands. Then something struck her. She saw a large, scary, white elephant's skull and bones. She ran in excitement to find her friend, Simba. 'Simba! Simba!' Kiara purred.

'What's wrong?' Simba replied, looking around in fright.

'Don't worry, it's just me,' she said calmly, 'how would you like to come on an adventure?'

'Where to?' he asked confused.

'Follow me and you will see.' Kiara said trying to convince him.

'Okay,' Simba said, jumping with excitement.

'Follow me Simba!' she said, already halfway down Pride Rock.

They ran excitedly and finally they got to the waterhole, they both lay down on the hot dry dirt and drank for a long time. After their drink they set off again on their long journey to the Elephant Graveyard.

They finally got to the graveyard and saw a huge elephant skull, they both stopped in horror. 'Wow! Cool!' they both whispered in happiness.

'Ha, ha!'

'What was that?'

Three large hyenas came out from inside the elephant's skull. 'Hello Pride-Landers,' they muttered in a crackly, scary voice.

'Run!' Simba whispered.

They both ran . . . woooh, they slipped down an elephant's ribcage. It was really bumpy. They ran and ran until they were safely back at Pride Rock.

What an amazing adventure!

Jessika Chloe Woodman (10)
Tatworth Primary School, Tatworth

A Day In The Life Of Shakespeare

Dear Elizabeth,
 Do you think you have ever seen a ghost? Lots of people think they have seen ghosts. I have seen many of them, for my habitat is the spirit world. It is not very entertaining, drifting around all day, staring at the terrifying mess of the cities. In my day, the streets of London were not exactly spotless, I admit, but pollution did not even exist! Oh yes, the good old days. Very old days in fact, the time of William Shakespeare. That's me.
 I have a few friends in the spirit world. They always call me Barnacle Bill or Billy Bones. I am not particularly fond of these silly nicknames, but I would not want to hurt my friends' feelings.
 I still carry on my job of writing plays. I ask some of the other spirits if they will be in my plays but they always say they have better things to do, like going to their homes when they were living or going to visit their graves and feel sorry for themselves. I, on the other hand, do not feel sorry for myself. My family hate me for dying. I am ashamed of myself.
 I often visit my old home or where it should be. I know that my family are long dead, but I cannot find them. They are probably in another country.
Oh I do wish you were real. I imagine you with deep chestnut hair and eyes like the sea after a storm. My love for you is strong, yet you are just a figment of my imagination.
 Wish you were real,
 Will Shakespeare.

Sofia Harrington (10)
Tatworth Primary School, Tatworth

A Day In The Life Of Thierry Henry

It was three days until the big match. The French and Arsenal striker Thierry Henry was preparing. At 4 o'clock he had landed in Portugal for Euro 2004. France's first game was against England. The team arrived at a private training ground and began training. The French captain Zinedine Zidane was talking to the team and explaining tactics. His threatening number seven rival captain, was David Beckham.

After Zinedine had finished talking to the team, he talked to me and co-striker, Trezuguet. These were his words . . .

'You,' he said, pointing a finger sharply at my chest, 'you play on the right and you,' he glared at Trezuguet, 'you play on the left. I want you to -' he pointed again, 'take both left and right corners. I myself will take the free kicks and Trezuguet will take the penalties. Get training,' he said.

As I walked onto the training ground I felt the breath of his shout scorching on my face as I sprinted casually onto the soft patterned grass. To my delight, the day was finally over.

When I woke up next morning, I could feel huge tension climbing my body as though a mountaineer was climbing Mount Everest. We trained hard that day and finally it was match day.

7.30pm seemed to be approaching rapidly and before I knew it, we were on the pitch.

It wasn't until the 31st minute that a goal came. Frank Lampard had headed the ball home for England and it was 1-0.

In the 87th minute, Captain Zidane scored a free kick. It was the 91st and a penalty to France. Zinedine took the penalty because Trezuguet was off.

Goal! Goal! France had won 2-1.

Mark Ricketts (10)
Tatworth Primary School, Tatworth

Dear Diary

19th January 1861
Dear Diary,
   My first day at the workhouse has already gone downhill, Master Rickman's a persecuting man, he has already shouted at me for sitting down and for having dirty hands!
   The place is intimidating and the cries in the night terrorise me. Those footsteps will be the woman who checks we are asleep, those girls had better still their cries!

20th January 1861
Dear Diary,
   School is terrible, for hours we repeated, 'God is love, God is good, God is just, God is holy.'
   I have thought about running away, the only thing that stops me is the shed in the yard. The only light in the shed falls through the barred window. Beaten every day until they're good - they are the girls who ran away, but were caught . . .

Later . . .
   I cannot believe it, I cannot believe my good fortune. Master Rickman has picked me to work down on the bottom floor to keep the fires burning! The gates are carelessly unlocked most of the day, if I could just slip out when everyone else is filling their buckets of coal . . .

21st January 1861
Dear Diary,
   You will not believe my good fortune. God is love, God is just, God is good, God is holy! I have escaped, I am free! Once free, I ran and ran. I didn't stop until I was far away from everything I knew. I don't know what will happen to me now but I am free from that place forever. I hope . . .

Holly Adeymo (10)
Tatworth Primary School, Tatworth

Evacuee

I was lying on the cold, damp floor knowing that one of these days I would have to leave my mum. I awoke to find my mum standing over me with an apple.

'Sorry son, you're going to live in the country.'

I stared at my mum chewing my apple.

'Hurry up, your train leaves in ten minutes.'

I packed my suitcase and looked at my mum.

Mum said, 'I'll take you down to the station.'

As the train pulled out of the station, I waved goodbye to my mum. As the train went round the corner, I settled back in my chair clutching my photo, gas mask and five shillings. The train rattled along. Just before I left my mum had told me to get off at Chard Station. I nearly fell asleep but just as I was dozing off, this tall man came in and said, 'Anything off the trolley, my son?'

'Yes please,' I said because I hadn't eaten since breakfast. I picked up a packet of sweets and a chocolate bar off the trolley.

'That will be a shilling plus the train fare, so that will be one and a half shillings.'

All of a sudden the train started coming off the rails, all the lights went out and I heard the lantern fall from the hook. Then the trolley came crashing down onto my leg and I heard a deafening crack.

To be continued . . .

James Orchard (10)
Tatworth Primary School, Tatworth

My Little Brother

My little brother Edward wakes up at 9.30, he is very lively. He pours the pint of water into his washbowl from the jug. Both the jug and washbowl are made of porcelain.

Edward washes himself by swishing water from the washbowl over his face. Then he gets dressed in his blouse, dungarees, trousers, his boots and his jacket. Meanwhile I am getting dressed in my headband, my boots, my dress and pinafore.

'Victoria, breakfast! Come down, you too Edward,' she called to me.

'Coming Mother,' I called back at the same time as Edward.

For breakfast I had nettle porridge and stale seasoned bread along with some cold tea, the same as Edward.

I ran out of the house and down the road to the milkman, who was using an old brass milkchurn and a ladle to get milk for me and Mother. Then I raced back home gave her the milk and ran all the way without stopping.

At school, Edward got the cane for fighting and I got a very strict warning from Mrs Hobbs the teacher, for looking down at my slate and breaking the nib on my slate-pencil. Just then (thankfully) the bell rang and I rushed outside to hoop and stick and played hoop for the rest of playtime.

Suddenly, 'Alert fire!' the teacher on duty shouted and quickly we ran to the field.

At home time I rushed to buy my favourite candy stick for one quart.

Nathalie L Knight (9)
Tatworth Primary School, Tatworth

It's Horrible!

I can't do it, it's horrible! Mum grounded me yesterday and it wasn't just no watching TV for a week. No going outside for a week; no it was far worse! There's going to be rotten food everywhere, dirty clothes . . . yes, I've got to clean my brother's room out! Yuck!

Ciara Reddington (11)
Threemilestone School, Truro

Me And My Mate

When we became friends...
    When I first walked into the classroom I knew she was going to be my friend. Olivia walked over and asked if I wanted to play with her. I said yes.
    School...
    As we grew up we were going over each other's houses. The first time she came over to my house, she wouldn't stop phoning her mum. We started drifting apart after a couple of years.

Meetings...
    My parents were wondering why I was so down. A couple of weeks later I found out what they were doing; they were planning a day trip to Plymouth for both of us. Shopping, lunch, ice-skating.

Future...
We have both left school, still friends of course. We text each other when we get time to. We meet. We even go on holiday together, every year to Ibiza.

Bryony Thomas (11)
Threemilestone School, Truro

A Day In The Life Of Salem

Salem was born in a home with an owner who sells kittens. When we went to pick Salem, we didn't know what to call him and then it hit me and I said, 'He's black, so let's call him Salem.' So my family thought about it and said, 'Yes!'

It was time for Salem to leave his mother. When we got home he was all purry and he came and sat on my lap and kept headbutting me. Later on, my brother came and took him away, Salem doesn't like Aaron and he runs off all the time.

About an hour later, Salem went missing because I left the door open and so Salem got out and was missing for a long while. We tried to call his name but it was no use because he didn't know his name properly yet.

When I got home from school Mum had a surprise, while she was in the garden she'd spotted Salem in a hole.

Soon Salem was old enough to go out, but when we let him out, he ran back in!

Naomi Rawlings (11)
Threemilestone School, Truro

A Day In The Life Of Tintin

A typical day in the life of Tintin is action-packed and adventurous.

Firstly, he practises his exercises with his pet dog Snowy. Then he sets off to see his friend Captain Haddock in his house Marlinspike Manor. This house is usually where Tintin's adventures begin. His adventures are often in different countries.

He often travels with his friend, the alcohol-addicted Captain Haddock. The deaf, albeit brilliant, Professor Calculus and the clumsy twins, Thompson and Thompson.

His adventures vary, sometimes kidnapping, sometimes smuggling, sometimes treason. But all the time it is exciting and at the end of his adventures he goes home to bed, ready for another day.

Sanjan Duttagupta (11)
Threemilestone School, Truro

Theme Park Disaster

My family and I were in the theme park - not an ordinary sort of theme park; a dark, scary black theme park. People around were chatting and it was getting very noisy. All of the rides were lit inside. There were people inside the rides, even the scary ones. Mum, Dad, Matthew and I were all walking around until suddenly I saw a ride, it didn't look like an ordinary ride, it looked big and scary.

'Mum!' I called out as the grey clouds floated over my head. 'Can I go on this ride, it's called Pirate Extravaganza?'

'Why don't we all go on it?' Mum answered. Everybody walked onto the dusty steps of the Pirate Extravanganza and took a seat. The seats looked nice and new, especially the back few. The ride had started and everything was going smooth until everything started going all bumpy . . . everything shuddered . . .

The ride stopped and there were crowds of people getting off, (everybody was shoving and barging about). Mum, Dad and Matthew had all got out. But I couldn't . . . I was glued to the seat, my seatbelt wouldn't undo; I was practically stuck there forever. Nobody knew. I was still on it and the ride had started again. Everybody thought that I'd just got onto it, but I hadn't!

Meanwhile, Mum, Dad and Matthew suddenly realised I was missing. What were they going to do? Matthew thought that I was probably still on the ride but who knows?

Sophie Hay (10)
Threemilestone School, Truro

The Worst Beach

June 7th

Today I had the worst day of my life at the beach. Firstly dogs came and stole my sausage off the barbecue; they're such a pain. So that then left me with no food; my brother got the first sausage before the dogs came along.

Secondly my tent fell down (and the dogs chewed it up) so once again there was another problem. This day couldn't get any worse, or could it?

Thirdly, a jellyfish stung me on the thigh. So my day did get worse; shortly after my brother ran out because fish were swimming around his feet. So I burst out with laughter. He couldn't laugh at me as he knew it would hurt me.

Lastly, the sun went in so we headed back home so that was the worst day of my life at the beach.

Olivia Baker (11)
Threemilestone School, Truro

Friendship

They're there for each other, day and night. When you're upset, along they come to comfort you. You can tell them your feelings, they always understand. Your secrets will be kept forever. Sometimes you may fall out, but you surely will make-up again. That's what friends were made for.

Jasmine Rose (10)
Threemilestone School, Truro

My Worst Nightmare

Oh great! My worst nightmare - it's ten past eleven. I wish it was ten past twelve. It could be terrible. The door is opening. I draw out my small pointed plastic stick from my big bag and my shield of paper . . .

I have to go into my first English lesson.

Danny Martin (10)
Threemilestone School, Truro

In Her Tent

Something was there in her tent. She could feel its hair across her face. Trying to be as discreet as possible, Morwena stretched her hand out and fumbled for her torch; she grabbed it and shone it at the 'thing'. Phew, it was Emily fumbling around to find her diary!

Wendy Matthews (11)
Threemilestone School, Truro

Lots Of Jokes

Last night was so freaky! My brother Will and his friends played the worst joke on me ever!

It began just before I fell asleep and my brother had all of his friends over, making it worse. They all knew I was into UFOs and aliens and things like that, but not after what he did.

Suddenly, as I was just falling asleep, a light started to appear through my bedroom door. It was so scary. As soon as the light stopped, shadows began to appear with the light. Shadows of aliens' spaceships. Then with no warning at all, music played as if they were warning me about something. But then I had an excellent idea.

I turned towards the door and guess who I saw? My brother and all his friends standing there, holding a torch; some string and a pot of flying saucer sweets! They had fooled me! At one point I did think there were real UFOs in our house.

Seeing as I couldn't get back to sleep, I stayed up all night with all the others to have a midnight feast and to help tell the ghost stories.

Meanwhile, in Mum and Dad's room, something was creeping through the window.

'Argh!'

'What was that?' I asked myself, but just laughed as I knew it was just one of Will's silly tricks again. After that time, I will never believe in flying saucers and aliens like that again! (Well, I don't think so!)

Milly Trevail (11)
Threemilestone School, Truro

Strange Invasion

'Boring!' Alex was in the Lake District and it was the most boring day of his life. He was sitting on a plaque at the top of Ben Nevis congratulating himself for getting to the top.

Alex was quiet with ginger hair and eyes. He loved spending time with his family but recently things weren't going well between his parents. His friends teased him but for once he could get away from the classroom and enjoy the countryside.

At Planet Wooves, the Woweys were planning to move to Earth. Their land was exploding in half an hour and everyone was getting frantic. The city was alive with tiny Waveys waddling around, trying to get things sorted.

They had a hydro rocket especially for emergencies. Everyone waddled into the pink giant. Be, Bo, Bon . . . the rocket had left home just in time to set off for its destination. In a few weeks it would be on the planet called Earth.

The planet could be seen now and they would be entering the atmosphere. Suddenly there was a bash and a bang. They had landed on Earth.

By now Alex's parents had reached the top of the mountain and they started to get out the different cheeses.

Alex jumped down from the plaque to see what it said. As he did he noticed a pink rocket on one of the letters. He picked it up in curiosity. It didn't look like anything exciting; so he threw it down the mountain.

'Rubbish these days!' tutted Alex.

Chloe Northover (11)
Threemilestone School, Truro

The Life Of My Amazing Guinea Pig

Moving house
   Frodo's amazing life really kicked off when he moved into his new home with me. He was 6 weeks old when I got him, he was very scared of me when we first got him. He was lucky because we also got a rabbit so he had a friend.

Pain in the back
   Frodo has been knocked about quite a lot of times, he has been dropped and hit by accident, but he was almost killed by the rabbit because the rabbit scratched his back up and he was on medication.

All grown up
   Frodo is now fully grown, he eats tonnes and can't say no to a daily nap!

Ross Pascoe (11)
Threemilestone School, Truro

The Visitor

The doorbell rang. I looked through the window and I saw green bogies, big spots, hairy moles, lots of hair and food in its teeth. Who was it? Mum opened the door. It was my uncle. Mum kissed the old monster, and guess what . . . I had to kiss him too!

Carly Maker (10)
Threemilestone School, Truro

Footsteps Following

The bus screeched to a halt and Sanchu clambered out. The snow floated down slowly from the dull grey sky, as she yanked down her hat. Her shoulders drooped and her head hung low as she fought her way into the screaming wind. It was a long traipse down the black lane to her home.

The flowers drooped sadly and the leaves rustled angrily as Sanchu stumbled down the lane. A gust of wind suddenly blew and Sanchu flew back. She looked down at her sodden school trousers, 'Mum will be furious!' she whispered to herself. Then she stopped. What was that?

With palms sweating and jaws chattering; Sanchu got to her feet. There was definitely someone or something there. She was sure. Overcome by panic Sanchu fumbled on. Then she halted. What should she do?

Suddenly her legs bolted back into action and she was speeding off down the lane. She was constantly aware of the footsteps speeding up as well. *Thump!* Sanchu could hear her heart beating. Suddenly, she flung her bag off her back and charged on around the corner. She could hear the footsteps following her . . .

'Stop!' a voice bellowed urgently.

Sanchu crept back around the corner. A bold, ugly man stood in front of her.

'Gosh, you can't half run fast!' he said smiling.

'Thanks,' Sanchu muttered bashfully in reply. 'Anyway, why were you trying to catch me?'

'Because you left your purse on the bus, and I was trying to catch you to give it back!'

Katie Bowen (11)
Threemilestone School, Truro

Don't Like Him

My hands were sweaty. I was nervous, I hate going to him. He stinks of wee. Wee from my dog. I'm waiting for him. He looks scary, scary like a werewolf going to eat your head. Trying to calm down, watching fish. The dentist calls my name . . . 'Peter please!'

Jake Eells (11)
Threemilestone School, Truro

Recount

I was sitting down on a bench in the park eating my most favourite strawberry ice cream at about 3.30pm. Lots of people were chatting and children played on the swings. I saw a man staring at all the people, but I didn't really take any notice until he started running. He caught my eye, and when he ran up to a dark-haired man, wearing a suit and grabbed his briefcase I started to take more notice of him.

The thief was about six foot six and about twenty-four years of age. He had short brown hair and had very big built muscles. He wore blue jeans and a light blue top with the name Quiksilver on it. He also wore black trainers with a green stripe down the side. He was alone.

The man was walking out of the park to his new, posh silver car. The man rushed over without looking at his face (but he knew what he looked like, seems he had been staring at the man). He didn't have time to hold onto the briefcase. The thief turned around and ran my way, he was coming closer to me. The man who'd had the briefcase shouted to the thief but he had gone.

I dropped my ice cream (how could I?) and started to run after him. I almost caught him when I fell over, but he sped off into the woods with the briefcase under his arms and head to his chest.

Janie Blair (11)
Threemilestone School, Truro

Mini Saga

I didn't want to go but I had to. It was the worst experience I'd ever had. I saw him coming. His cross, red eyes, his white, bald head, his wrinkly face, his giant, crooked nose, his dull suit. I hate being sent to the head teacher's room.

Daniel Wiltshire (11)
Threemilestone School, Truro

A Day In The Life Of A Horse

We were next, I couldn't let her down now we'd got so far. What would she do if I couldn't make a jump?

It was our turn, I couldn't move, I was stuck stiff, I was so scared. What should I do? I started to panic. She gripped the reins around my neck and started kicking me in the side. I had to go. At first a trot, then a canter, and then the gallop.

We were getting closer and closer to the first jump. We'd made it and the second and the third. We were heading for the hardest and the last jump. Nobody had made this jump in the competition, if we did we would win. My muscles tensed up as we reached the jump. We made it, we had won the competition, we had beaten the other jockeys, some of the best in the world.

Later on that evening, she let me out of my stable and I cantered in the sunset. I was so pleased with myself for winning that race. I will never forget it, I promise!

Hannah Finney (11)
Trannack CP School, Helston

A Day In The Life Of A Penny

'Gosh it's squashed in here, you would not believe it, and it's practically hotter than Spain.'

Oh sorry, I forgot to introduce myself, I am a penny! Yes, I know you've heard those stupid rumours that pennies don't talk and they definitely don't come alive, but I am glad to say they are utterly and completely not true. I came alive about 2 years ago and have travelled the world. I think I started off in a factory somewhere and ended up with this happy bunch in the local newsagents in Helston. Hopefully I will travel the world again someday but we, I mean I, will have to wait and see.

'Right then, that will be a penny change,' says Mrs Thomas, the owner of this place.

Oh no, here comes the hand, the hand which decides all, oh she's coming close, even closer. Yes! She picks me up so now I am off on my whirlwind adventure of the world.

2 days have passed and so far I have been in a newsagent and in a café in London, a coffee machine, and I am now on my way to London Airport.

Oh look, here comes his hand, oh yes, what, ow! Wow! I'm in a drain, oh well, ever heard the saying, 'see a penny and pick it up, all day long you'll have good luck'? Well I don't think that will be happening with me! Oh well!

Lottie Thompson (11)
Trannack CP School, Helston

A Day In The Life Of A Pet Mouse

I woke with a sudden craving for jam, I scrambled to my paws sniffing and smelling as I went. I then dug my way through the thick layer of sandy shavings, searching for food. My nose suddenly twitched, I sat up, and my body was motionless. My brain buzzed, as I tried to work, out what was going on! Suddenly I felt a sharp pinch on my tail. I squeaked with fright. I suddenly felt myself being lifted higher and higher! My feet suddenly touched ground, except it was not sweet-smelling like my home, oh no, this ground was much the opposite! It had a harsh smell hanging around it, a bit like old cheese. If this was the dream moon . . . I mean I knew it was made out of cheese but it didn't have to have gone-off. I'm . . . wait, hold on, rewind, rewind. Let's just think logically here . . . calm down, Eve!

Just then the ground lowered me into the soft bedding of shavings; I was safe in my home! Then I heard a soft scratching, I plodded to the noise with curiosity. Then I saw that sitting in the corner, snuffling quietly, was a young mouse. My eyes were fixed on the tiny, furry figure. I did not know what to say, but at least I had a friend!

Olivia Tunstall (11)
Trannack CP School, Helston

Treasure

Bump! 'What's this?' I had landed on something cold and wooden. I looked down to my feet at a box, a key, a treasure chest. I used the key to open the chest and to my amazement I saw pearls, rubies, gold necklaces, silver and bronze earrings and lots more.

Alice Furness (10)
Trannack CP School, Helston

A Day In The Life Of Dobby

Dobby woke up this morning thinking, *no not another day at school. I just can't wait for the school holidays.* As you've probably guessed, he doesn't like school, he gets bullied, he hates school.

Then the school bell went, it was the school holidays. Dobby jumped out of his seat and shouted, 'Yes, holidays at last!'

'Sorry to spoil your fun, but there's some homework,' the teacher mumbled.

On the way home he met the school bully, Tom Totskin.

'Dobby, what are you doing?'

'Um, um nothing, just going home.'

'What, going home to Mummy? Mummy's boy.'

'Well at least I'm not a bully.'

'I'm not a bully!'

Well, there is some truth in that,' said Tom's best friend, Mike.

'Do you want to come over?'

'Yeah sure Liam.'

'You didn't call me Dobby, yes!'

That night Liam could not sleep with excitement.

After that Liam was the most popular boy in school. And the rest is history.

Victoria Martins (10)
Trannack CP School, Helston

A Day In The Life Of An Elephant

'Gosh!' I must have grown, I'm huge . . . I'm an *elephant.*'

Jake (very surprised that he was an elephant) started to explore the jungle he didn't recall going to.

Suddenly Jake heard a loud bang. He plodded, as fast as his fat legs could carry him, over to behind a bush (which wasn't really a good place for an elephant to hide). From behind the bush Jake could see some suspicious-looking men with guns, they were hunters. Jake charged over to a much wider bush and lay down so that the hunters could not see trunk or tail of him.

The hunters carried on trying to capture and shoot Jake until the afternoon of the seventy hour long day, but they just couldn't capture him until the hunters thought ahead and dug a big pit and put some peanuts on the opposite side of the pit that Jake would be approaching.

When Jake arrived next to the pit, he went to get the peanuts. He lost his balance and fell. The hunters ran out from their hiding place and were going to shoot him and use his tusks for ivory when . . .

Jake woke up, it was all a dream. 'Phew, thank goodness that was only a dream.'

After recovering from shock, Jake went and told his mum about his dream.

Megan Jones (10)
Uphill Primary School, Uphill

A Day In The Life Of An Actress

Hi, I'm Louise, a ten-year-old *famous* actress but I don't like to boast okay? Well a little boasting is alright from time to time if that's okay with you? Anyway, I live in a huge house with a theatre in it and outside I have lots of fields with my three horses, Buttercup, Crystal and Blaze. I live happily with my mum, dad and little sister (my big bro moved out two years ago). Well that's me and my family covered so I'll tell you my story of why I now keep my diary *all* the time!

I was really happy because I had made a breakthrough, I had been the star of a show and everyone *loved* me! I was so happy I spent the rest of our 100 hour day celebrating with lots of Coke and lemonade, yum-yum! But after that people wanted me in their plays and a very good director offered me a part in 'Ghost Watch' in America on the 5th May and I accepted the part of the young girl (the heroine). I was so happy that I was better known that I forgot about keeping up my diary.

The next day I was in town when another famous director asked me to act an important girl part in a play called 'Mother Love' in Australia on the 5th May as well and because I wasn't keeping up my diary, I accepted (I am so stupid sometimes). So I was eager to learn the words and I was getting really good at them when I looked at the front of both and realised the mistake I'd made because they were both on the *same day!* Oops! I panicked, trying to decide which to do, for a minute I wanted to do 'Ghost Watch' and the next minute I wanted to do 'Mother Love', I just couldn't choose!

I went to see my dad and he said he couldn't help me and that I should have kept my diary but I would just have to learn the hard way, (he was helpful, now wasn't he?). So then I went to my sister who said, 'Time machine,' which gave me an idea that would save my career! I remembered about the different time zones! If I quickly flew to America in my jet, I could do the play and then quickly fly to Australia then I'd be in time for both!

So it all worked out and I was brilliant (sorry, about the boasting), I was superb! And *now* I always keep my diary and I always will!

Belinda Hill (10)
Uphill Primary School, Uphill

A Day In The Life Of Wayne Rooney

I was one of the top goal scorers of Euro 2004. I got England into the quarter finals of Euro 2004 but I had to go off because I was injured - but the really bad thing was that England lost.

I'm the youngest player for England and I'm an attacker alongside Michael Owen. I've been playing for England now for about eighteen months. I have enjoyed it a lot and now I'm one of England's best players.

I can't wait for next season, it will be exciting and a challenge for me. I'm going to try my best and have fun. I've been offered to Chelsea and I will have a contract worth millions. I probably will go to Chelsea.

My aim for next year is to be the top goal scorer for England. But I'm up against some top-class players. I hope I do well in the World Cup 2006. I have met loads of new friends as well.

This is a great job which I'm doing. All of that practise went to good use now that I'm doing my dream job.

Charlie Williams (10)
Uphill Primary School, Uphill

A Day In The Life Of Vi Jay Singh

It was a nice sunny day at the golf course and I will be playing golf in the PGA Tour 2004.

I teed off at the first with my driver and I was pleased with my shot because it went far and it was really straight down the fairway.

I took my 7 iron out of my bag but I hit it too far so I had a bit of stress, but I had a lot of back spin on the ball and it went into the hole. I didn't see it go in but I walked on to the green and I couldn't find my ball, so I looked in the hole and it was in there! I threw my ball into the crowd.

When I walked to the next hole it started to rain and then it started to thunder and all of the players on the course had gone off. We stayed off the course for five hours and then we gave up, it didn't stop raining and thundering. We have to play again next year.

Alex Fry (10)
Uphill Primary School, Uphill

A Day In The Life Of A Pop Star

There was once a young girl called Sally. She was just a normal girl who loved to sing. One day she thought it would be nice to join a choir. This helped Sally's singing very much. She loved it, she went with all the other children to different places to sing. Later in the year she saw a poster saying 'Talent Show'. She thought she was very good at singing now, so she entered.

On the night, Sally was very nervous but she tried her hardest and the judges gave her nine out of ten. Sally was very pleased and guess what? She won! She got a lovely golden trophy and after the show a young man called Tim came up to her, he thought she was very good and asked her if she would sing at a disco, Sally agreed very happily.

The next week she went to the Village Hall all glammed up and ready to go. When she got there, her nerves started to play up because there were so many people there and something even worse happened - Sally forgot all her words! But Tim knew what to do, he projected them on to a screen at the back of the hall. Sally thought it was a really good idea and she sang really well and after that she got a record deal and became very famous.

Zoe Scott (10)
Uphill Primary School, Uphill

A Day In The Life Of Trampoline Man

I went down to the park to go on the trampolines. Everyone calls me 'trampoline man' I can't remember my real name! All my friends ask me to do loads of tricks then they ask me to teach them but I say I can't be bothered. My teacher said I should go in for a competition, she said that I would come first, but I didn't want to. The next day was my birthday and my gran gave me a chain that was meant to give you confidence.

So I went to the competition. I was fifth to go, so I got on the trampoline feeling nervous. I looked in my pocket for the chain but it wasn't there so I jumped off and ran away to find my chain.

My friends wanted to help so they put their money together to buy a new one and they told me to look in my sock drawer where they'd put the chain. I looked in there and it was my chain! So they got a cab and we went to the competition as fast as the cab would go.

We got there just in time for the end and I went last and I won a massive trophy.

Then I went home and put it on the mantelpiece, the next day I called my friends round for a surprise - I gave them a trophy each for helping me out. So I reckon they are the winners more than me.

Huw Morgan (10)
Uphill Primary School, Uphill

The Day In The Life Of A Young Child

Missy longed for some kind of friend, but not a human friend, Missy wanted a pet. Her mum and her stepdad did not think she was ready yet, because Missy was only eight years old. Missy however thought that she was ready and pleaded, 'I am, I am, please let me have a pet.' Missy pleaded so much that her mum gave in and said that they would go to the pet store and find a pet.

Missy decided that she would like a little Cocker Spaniel. It was golden all over with white specks. When Missy got home with her mum and her dog, her stepdad went out to buy some dog treats. Missy decided she would call her new dog Princess, because she looked like one.

When Missy's stepdad got back, they packed a picnic and went for a walk along the beach. Missy started to get hungry so they started their picnic. When Princess had finished her treats she started eating the sandwiches. When they had finished they went back home and as it was only seven o'clock, they went up to the park for an hour, then they had tea and went to bed.

In the morning Missy got up and went to school. When she got home she took Princess for a walk then came home and fell asleep, she was so happy!

Lizzie Duran (9)
Uphill Primary School, Uphill

A Day In The Life Of An Actress

One bright sunny morning I had an important phone call. It was a man and he was going to be directing a film which he wanted me to be in. So I got dressed and went to the set of the film. When I got there, I was in an empty room. Over in the corner, I found some cheerleading equipment. The director came over to me and told me about the film.

I soon found myself in a cheerleading outfit with pom poms in my hands. I felt really stupid. I had to do a scene where the cheerleaders were looking for someone to join the team. The director called, 'Action!' and we all went to our places. When we had done that scene, we went on to the next.

The next scene was one of the cheerleaders' competitions and this competition was upsetting because they lost. I had to do a temple with other girls and I had to go in the second row. I was really worried because a girl called Louise had to stand on my shoulders. Then the director called, 'Action!' I suddenly felt sick.

When it was time for the next scene I had to wear a golden, shiny outfit. I thought this scene was exciting. This scene was the final competition and the cheerleaders came in second! The director called, 'Action!' for the last time and we did the last scene.

I never forgot that day and soon I was hoping to be in another film.

Bonny Owens (10)
Uphill Primary School, Uphill

The Romans March To Battle

Clank! Clank! The fight is at full. I am as tired as a sloth. As frightened as a mouse and as hot as a volcano. I am a Roman and I am marching into battle.

Two hours later I'm standing in rubble. But I, Julius Caesar, have won the battle.

Patrick Cannon (9)
Widecombe-in-the-Moor Primary School, Newton Abbot